BENVOLIO

Benvolio

EMILY WHITAKER

TATE PUBLISHING
AND **ENTERPRISES**, LLC

Benvolio
Copyright © 2015 by Emily Whitaker. All rights reserved.

No part of this publication may be reproduced, stored in a retrieval system or transmitted in any way by any means, electronic, mechanical, photocopy, recording or otherwise without the prior permission of the author except as provided by USA copyright law.

This novel is a work of fiction. Names, descriptions, entities, and incidents included in the story are products of the author's imagination. Any resemblance to actual persons, events, and entities is entirely coincidental.

The opinions expressed by the author are not necessarily those of Tate Publishing, LLC.

Published by Tate Publishing & Enterprises, LLC
127 E. Trade Center Terrace | Mustang, Oklahoma 73064 USA
1.888.361.9473 | www.tatepublishing.com

Tate Publishing is committed to excellence in the publishing industry. The company reflects the philosophy established by the founders, based on Psalm 68:11,
"The Lord gave the word and great was the company of those who published it."

Book design copyright © 2015 by Tate Publishing, LLC. All rights reserved.
Cover design by Samson Lim
Interior design by Gram Telen

Published in the United States of America

ISBN: 978-1-68164-514-8
Fiction / Romance / General
15.07.29

1

As he stepped out of bed, the marble floor felt cool to Benvolio's feet. With his eyes mostly shut, he reached for his wooden sword and dragged it behind him into the hall, down the corridor, and into his cousin's room.

"Romeo, are you awake?" Benvolio said as he entered.

Romeo mirrored Benvolio. Both were still somewhat asleep, their bare feet cringing against the cold floor, wooden swords in hand. Their nightclothes hung off them, making them look smaller than they truly were.

"Yes, I'm awake," Romeo said.

"Can we practice dueling?"

"We're still in our nightclothes, Ben."

"Oh, right."

Benvolio slowly walked back to his room. He began to wake up properly as he dressed. The room was new to him. He had only been living with his cousin for a month after the passing of his parents due to a sickness that ran through his small village. Benvolio could not think of another place he would rather be. In his ten years of life, his happiest memories were with his cousin, in his home.

And a grand home it was. Built of stone, it sat strong and wide. Tall towers stood at the edges to look over the family's land, and large windows hung in every room, giving the villa a feeling of warmth. Named after its family, Montague villa was home to Romeo, his parents, and a number of serving men and women. It sat on the hills on the west side of Verona, Italy, a large village at the foot of the Italian Alps. The villa was the gateway to the Montague family business, opening up to rows of olive trees and acres of vineyards. It was a business that made the Montagues one of the most prominent, rich, and powerful families in Verona, second only to the Capulets.

Benvolio heard Romeo leave his room, walk down the hall, and stomp down the stairs. He wanted to catch up with him, so he didn't bother to fasten his boots or button his vest. He had given up on his unruly mop of brown hair a long time ago. It was going to do what it was going to do, and today it was standing up a bit in the front and extrafloppy all around. He grabbed his wooden sword and ran down the stairs.

"Breakfast is outside this morning, Master Benvolio," a serving woman said to him as he passed her in the hall.

Benvolio ran out to the courtyard. The sun was already warm and made it a bit easier to wake up. His eyes adjusted, and the sight was comforting. Romeo was sitting at a small table with his parents. On top of the table were fresh fruits, cheeses, freshly squeezed orange juice, and Benvolio's favorite, sweet braided bread covered in honey and nuts.

"Come join us, son," Lord Montague said. "You'll need your strength. From what I hear, you're practicing for a wild duel." He chuckled.

Benvolio took his seat at the table. Lady Montague smiled at him and offered him the sweet bread. He took it and covered his plate with piles of fruits and cheeses, and he took a big swig of his juice. With a full mouth, he quietly listened to his uncle speak of the family business. Plans to leave the business to Romeo and Benvolio were always on his uncle's mind. Benvolio tried to listen, but it was a beautiful morning, and he was full of energy, so he found it hard to do so.

"Go on then, you two," his uncle said with a jolly laugh. "Go play."

Benvolio took one last bite of his bread and shoved a few berries in there as well. He picked up his sword and took his fencing stance, facing Romeo. "Have at thee," he called out, managing to keep all the food in his mouth.

Romeo took his stance, and they slowly went through their moves. The clank of their wooden swords was matched only by the cheers and claps of Lord and Lady Montague.

"Well done, boys," Lady Montague said.

She rose from her seat and went to them. They held their swords to their sides because they knew what she was about to do. She walked to Benvolio and pushed his mop of hair away from his face. She then smiled and kissed him on his forehead. She did the same to Romeo, only kissing him on both cheeks and squeezing him tight until he squeaked. With a laugh, she messed up his perfect hair and went inside.

"You've got a hair out of place," Benvolio said.

"I do?" Romeo said, dropping his sword as he tried desperately to fix it.

Benvolio laughed. "Let's find Balthazar and teach him how to duel," he said.

Romeo led them back inside to the great sitting room, where they found Balthazar polishing the silver on the shelves surrounding the hearth. Since he was standing on a shaky stool, Balthazar had to catch his balance when they came running toward him. Benvolio cringed.

"Balthazar," Romeo said. "Watch what we learned at the First House in fencing."

Balthazar continued to polish as he watched. He was the same age as the boys, only he was the son of Lord Montague's valet, which meant he was up, dressed, fed, and working by the time Benvolio stepped out of bed every morning. Balthazar and his father were new to Verona and happy for the work. It didn't take long for the boys to befriend Balthazar. Although the friendship was blessed by Lord Montague, Benvolio overheard Balthazar's father telling him to make sure his chores never suffered. Benvolio had trouble understanding this and was frustrated when Balthazar couldn't play. Happy to include him while he worked, Benvolio took his stance in the middle of the great sitting room, and Romeo did the same.

"This is called the passado," Romeo said as he lunged toward Benvolio. "Punto reverso," he said, blocking Benvolio's backhand thrust. "Hey!" Romeo yelled with his killing blow to the side of Benvolio's chest.

Benvolio grabbed Romeo's wooden sword and put it under his armpit. Spinning in place, Benvolio fell onto the sitting couch and pulled the pillows down with him as he fell to the ground. With a dramatic gasp for air and his tongue hanging out of his mouth, he turned his head and said, "I die."

"Noooooooo!" Romeo pretended to cry to the gods.

"Romeo, you're supposed to be happy that you killed him," Balthazar said from his stool. "You're not supposed to cry after you win a fight."

"Oh," Romeo said. He pulled his wooden sword from Benvolio's armpit.

"Boys," Lord Montague said as he walked into the room. "Boys, when I told you to play, I meant outside. You need to understand that Balthazar has work to do and does not need to be interrupted by you. And he doesn't need you two

Emily Whitaker

messing up the work he has already done. Both of you pick up this mess and go outside."

Benvolio looked around and realized he had made a mess, but a dramatic death was messy. He began to pick up the pillows with Romeo's help. Lord Montague took a seat by the window and tried to read the daily sales reports.

"Lord Montague," Balthazar's father, Augustus, said as he came into the great sitting room.

Augustus gave Benvolio and Romeo a look of confusion as they were doing the job he probably felt his son should be doing. But when Augustus looked at Lord Montague, he dropped the subject.

"Sir," Augustus said, "I'm heading to the market myself today. Is there anything, in addition to your daily needs, that I can get for you?"

"You can bring these boys with you, please. They need to get outside, and I can't seem to get them there."

"Yes, sir. Boys, we will leave for the market in two minutes."

Benvolio fluffed the last pillow and placed it carefully on the couch as Romeo tossed another there.

"Come on, Balthazar, come with us," Romeo said.

With the last of the silver still in his hands, Balthazar looked to Lord Montague.

"Yes, Balthazar," Lord Montague said with a chuckle. "I meant you as well."

Balthazar put the silver back on the hearth and jumped down to meet the boys. Benvolio wrapped his arm around Balthazar's shoulders and pulled him out of the room.

"We're going to teach you all the fighting moves we know," Benvolio said.

"You'll make a great sword fighter," Romeo added.

As they came over the hill into town, the market was sitting under a cloud of kicked-up dirt. Benvolio kicked the dirt at his feet to contribute as he listened to Romeo tell Balthazar everything they knew about fencing. And in case Romeo missed anything, Benvolio was ready to speak up.

Augustus led them quickly into the crowd, so Benvolio pushed the chatty boys to keep up with him. They stopped at the baker's, Benvolio's favorite shop. The baker greeted Benvolio by name as Benvolio took a deep breath of the thick smell of bread cooling beside the ovens. From there, they headed to the meat market. Benvolio kept his nose hidden. The smell was growing sourer with the rising sun. He stared at the dead chickens hanging upside down—some with feathers, some without—and the red meats sitting in salts that were turning a strange gray around the edges. The crowd swarmed around him and pushed him away from Augustus. He gave up and let the crowd win. He left the meat stand and turned to join Romeo and Balthazar, who were standing beside the market's center fountain. The soft breeze pushed through the water of the fountain and sprayed them with a cool mist.

"Let's practice then," Romeo said. "We'll show Balthazar the moves." He raised his wooden sword, and they began. "It's more like a dance than a fight, isn't it?"

"I suppose," Benvolio said.

"No, it's not," Balthazar said, watching their every move.

"Sure, it is," Romeo said. "Think about it. We learn our steps like we do in a dance. Watch, Ben has his part, and I have mine. When we do the move together, we move together, add the passion of the fight to raise the swords, and see? It's like a dance."

Benvolio smiled. "You can find something beautiful in everything, Romeo."

He raised his sword to block Romeo's, and from their wooden swords came a metal clank. The boys froze. Benvolio turned back to the meat market to see a crowd forming.

"It's a real fight," Balthazar said. "Let's go watch."

The boys ran into the crowd. Balthazar pushed past Benvolio. When Benvolio made it to the center of the crowd, he saw Balthazar stop beside his father, who was on his knees at the foot of an angry tall woman. Her sharp dagger pointed at Augustus's throat. She was dressed as a proper lady, in a black dress that shimmered blue when she moved in the sunlight. Her black hair was pulled back so tight her skin stretched. Her eyebrows twisted on her face, and she spat as she spoke.

"Montague slave," she called Augustus. "Dirt-wielding scum."

Benvolio knew she was from the Capulet family, and the hatred she was spewing for his family's name had bloodied the streets of Verona for over a century. But this was the first time Benvolio had ever seen the fight for himself. He could never get his uncle to tell him what the fight was about. Every time he asked about it, he was told to take great pride in his name and never allow a filthy Capulet to tell him otherwise. He was told the Capulets were evil and angry people, and then he was told never to fear them.

Benvolio felt there was a kind of peace to Augustus's response to Lady Capulet's anger. He was sitting on his knees, his eyes forward. He did not engage her. He simply let her yell. Benvolio was sure Augustus had done nothing wrong except wear the colors of the Montague family crest.

Beside the Lady Capulet stood a girl. She had to be Benvolio's age. Her dark hair and dark dress matched her mother's. She was a Capulet, but her anger was different. Her porcelain cheeks were covered in tears and dust.

"That's enough," she yelled out to her mother. "Please stop."

Lady Capulet turned and slapped the girl with the back of her hand, which was busy with rings. Benvolio watched as the girl's strength didn't bend. As she looked back at her mother, he saw her whisper something that put a look of terror on her mother's face. The girl stepped back to dodge another blow, and then she turned and ran away.

Emily Whitaker

Without hesitation or a word to Romeo, Benvolio took off after her. As he passed her mother, he heard her scream out, "You will do no such thing, young lady!"

Benvolio kept running after the girl. He ran hard, but she was running harder. He tried to call out to her, but he couldn't catch his breath, so he just kept running. She was headed toward the church, but she passed it. She ran around it to the west side. Afraid he was going to lose her, he sped up as much as he could. His heart was pounding, and he wondered if it was the running that made it pound so hard or if it was her. He had never found a reason to run this fast before. He raced around the church and saw the dark of her dress head into the sycamore grove. He entered the grove and kept his eyes on her as she leapt and swerved through the trees like a doe. Benvolio was not as graceful. The roots of the trees jutted up out of the ground, grabbing his toes; and the branches that hung low slapped his cheeks as he passed through them. She started to slow down so she could take down her tightly pulled-back hair. It fell and rested on her shoulders. Her dark hair was gold in the sunlight. She was beautiful. Then she was gone.

Benvolio could see nothing but dirt; he could taste nothing but dirt. His chest felt empty as he rolled over and gasped for air. His feet were still stuck on the root he had fallen over. The twisted trees made him dizzy as they danced above him.

"Are you all right?"

Her face came into focus as she put her hand out to help him up.

"Sit here," she said. "It might not be a good root to jump over, but it makes a great seat."

She placed him on the root, and as he began to catch his breath, he wished he was still on the ground, where the earth was cool on his head and he was not so dizzy. He breathed deeply, and eventually the dizziness began to fade. He looked up at her. She was standing beside him, watching him with a worried look on her face. She smiled at him and brushed off the dirt from his chest. He stopped breathing again, and the dizziness came back.

"Orange and red crest," she said, looking at the patch on his vest. "Such warm colors the Montague family has." She sat beside him. "I'm a Capulet." She made her dress shimmer emerald in the sunlight.

Benvolio smiled.

"You were in the market just now, weren't you?" she asked him.

He nodded.

"Was that your manservant?"

"It was," he managed. "You stood up for him? Why did you do that?"

"My name is Rosaline. What's yours?"

"Benvolio."

"Benvolio Montague." She let the name sit for a moment. "My mother is very serious about her feelings

Emily Whitaker

for the Montagues. Even my uncle, the head of our family, doesn't care for the fight as much as her. I don't really get it at all." She turned to him. "I'm supposed to hate you."

"I know. I'm supposed to hate you too."

"But you can't, can you?" She smiled at him. "You can't figure out how to hate me just because you're told to."

"I can't."

Benvolio was starting to catch his breath again. It was easy to talk to her. He leaned back against the trunk of the tree and played with a stick, picking at it and tossing the bits around. He watched her as she got comfortable on the root. He was happy to see that she had nowhere else she would rather be.

"Your dress has some mud on the hem," he said. He took a piece of the hem to see if he could rub it off with his sleeve.

"I think I like it better that way," she said, taking a handful of her dress and examining it. "Brown, the color of earth. It's a warm color too. It's the color of your eyes."

She smiled at Benvolio, and again he felt dizzy. She bent down and took a handful of dirt, straightened out the skirt of her dress, and spread the dirt all over it. "I like it much better this way, don't you?" she asked.

"I really do," he said, laughing.

"Help me then."

She took another glob of dirt from the ground and offered it to Benvolio. He put his hand out to her, and she

Benvolio

dropped the glob on his hand. She took up a handful for herself and began to rub it all over her dress.

"Come on, then. Help me," she said.

Benvolio reached out, took her skirt, and wiped the mud on it. She started to laugh, and Benvolio looked at her. He had seen her cry and seen her in pain, and now, more than anything, he wanted to see her face as she laughed.

"Your eyes, they're green," he said to her, confused.

"Are they?"

"When you helped me up, they were blue."

"And so was I, but now I'm happy."

"Your eyes change color with your mood?"

"Guess what color they are when I'm mad?"

"I…I don't know."

She hopped off the root and did a little twirl for Benvolio to show how the muddy dress looked. "What do you think?" she asked.

"Much better. You've got mud in your hair."

"We'll call it an accessory," she said. She reached out her hand. "Come on, then. Walk me home. Or at least walk me out of the woods, and then don't let my mother see you. I wouldn't want her to give you all the credit for my new dress."

"Rosaline?" he said, liking the feel of her name as it rolled off his tongue.

"Yes?"

"What did you say to your mother right before you ran off?"

"Why? Was she horrified?"

"She was."

"I told her I was going to tell Mother Superior at the convent what she was doing. I heard my mother speaking to her once about the fight between our families. Mother Superior said that any soul who participated in the fight would be damned to hell. I saw my mother laugh at her, but I could tell she was terrified. So I whispered to her that I was going to tell Mother Superior, who is going to tell God what she was doing."

"Why didn't you?"

"Because if the church could stop this fight, don't you think they would have by now? There is no point. Our families have hated each other for so long we don't even remember why. The fear of God can't stop it now."

"What about the grace of God?"

She put out her hand to Benvolio once more. "Are you going to walk me home or not, Benvolio Montague?"

He smiled and took her hand, and together they walked through the woods. She showed him a path she had made that led them to the wall of the Capulet villa at the edge of her family's land.

"Will you be all right?" Benvolio asked her. "I mean, will your mother be angry with you about your dress? Will she still be angry about what happened in the market?"

Rosaline stopped walking. She looked at the wall of her home in silence for a moment, then turned to Benvolio. "Do you see that tree down there that reaches over the villa wall?" she asked.

"I do," Benvolio said.

"On the other side of the wall stands another tree. The two reach out for each other because a wall has been built between them. Sometimes I climb the tree on the inside of the wall and swing over to its mate. Then I escape the walls of my home and play in the sycamore grove. Would you like to meet me in the grove again tomorrow night?"

"I would like that very much," he said.

"Then I'll meet you on the root you tripped over. Tomorrow night, when the moon is in the height of the night's sky, leave your home and come into the woods. I'll be there every night from now until eternity, and you can join me whenever you please. You're not afraid of the woods at night, are you?"

"No," he said. At least he wasn't until she said something.

"Good. Then I'll see you again tomorrow."

And with a kiss on his cheek, she ran out of the woods. Benvolio couldn't move. He tried to feel her lips on his cheek for as long as he could, but as she disappeared through the Capulet gates, so did the kiss. He took a deep breath and looked around. The day was getting old. Romeo was probably worried sick, wondering where he had gone. And Augustus, what had happened to him after he left?

Emily Whitaker

Benvolio hiked out of the woods and, turning away from the Capulet villa, ran home as fast as he could.

~

"I covered for you," Romeo said with a smile. "Did you catch her?"

"Did I catch who?" Benvolio asked.

"Come on, we need to wash up for supper."

Benvolio followed Romeo upstairs. He was planning to head straight to his room to wash up, but Romeo pushed him into his room instead.

"Tell me everything. Last I saw, you were running after that beautiful girl who stood up to whom I assume was her mother. Who is she? She was magnificent. Did you hold her while she cried? What happened?" Romeo asked. He had a sparkle in his eye, like he did every time he spoke of love.

"Is Augustus all right?" Benvolio asked, trying to buy himself a moment to think.

Benvolio shared everything with his cousin, and as badly as he wanted to tell Romeo of his feelings for Rosaline, for a Capulet, he couldn't do it. The words wouldn't come out of him. There was something very strong inside him that felt it was better to keep her a secret. To keep her all to himself.

"Augustus is doing fine now," Romeo said. "After you left, the prince's men came and stopped the woman. She was sent home, and Augustus was able to continue about his

Benvolio

day. He acted like nothing ever happened. But something happened to you. You ran after her with such passion. Did you help her? Was your love for her enough to take away her pain?"

"I didn't catch her. She ran into the church and straight to the nunnery. I thought it was best to leave her alone, so I went for a long walk in the sycamore grove."

"You hate it in there. You always fall. Well, maybe one day we will find out who she is, and you can confess your love for her."

"She is a Capulet," Balthazar said, coming into the room with a bowl full of warm water and a clean rag. "She is the daughter of the woman who attacked my father. They are both Capulets."

"But she stood up to her mother," Romeo said. "She tried to stop her."

"She is still a Capulet."

"And your father is still a servant, even though he conducted himself like a gentleman today. Why do you put so much power in a name?" Romeo said.

Balthazar was silent, and so was Benvolio. Romeo never spoke of the fight between the families, but it was clear he didn't put weight on the words that forced them to hate the Capulets either. However, even knowing this, Benvolio didn't feel like sharing what had happened with Rosaline in the woods. He joined Romeo at the bowl of warm water and dunked his hands in. Immediately the water turned brown, and he smiled at the memory of covering Rosaline's dress with mud.

"How many times did you fall in the grove, Benvolio?" Romeo said. "Disgusting." He dried his hands with the clean cloth, then tossed the cloth to Benvolio. "Come on, I'm starving."

2

Benvolio checked in with the moon every night for six years, confirming it was time again to meet Rosaline in the sycamore grove. And even when the moon wasn't in the sky, he would hike into the sycamore grove to meet her. He didn't need to look out his window anymore to know it was time, but he still did. The moon had hit its peak in the dark sky. It was full and oddly close, and he knew it would light up the grove and color Rosaline's dark hair with stripes of blue.

Grabbing his boots and a napkin full of dinner rolls, Benvolio blew out all the candles lighting his room and headed for the door. He silently closed his door behind him. The hall was dark and empty; even the servants had gone to bed for a moment's rest. He headed for the stairs, his feet soaking up the cool of the stone floor as he shuffled past Romeo's room, where he stopped. He put his head to the door to try to hear a sound.

"Romeo?" he whispered.

There was no answer. Romeo wasn't in his room, and he hadn't been for many nights now. He would come home in the daylight, shutting the sun out of his room and answering to no one. Benvolio knew Romeo was heartbroken. This wasn't the first time, but it was the only time he hadn't come to Benvolio for comfort.

As he softly turned and ran down the stairs, Benvolio promised himself that he would bring Romeo out into the sun tomorrow. He knew it would help because there was nowhere more beautiful than Verona on a hot summer's day—except, of course, the sycamore grove on a hot summer's night.

Jumping down the last few steps, Benvolio turned and wrapped around to the kitchen. He loved the smell of the kitchen when it was resting after a day of cooking. The herbs and spices took over the air, always making his stomach growl. He silently opened the back door, grabbed his napkin full of dinner rolls, and tossed them to the three hunting dogs staring up at him, licking their chops. After his first night of sneaking out years ago, he learned to bring the dogs a roll to keep them from barking, and it didn't take long for them to learn to expect it. Now they would sit obediently, waiting for him to come out with their treat. They devoured the rolls in seconds and turned to Benvolio with their big eyes, ears back, and tails wagging.

"That's all I have for you," he said.

He reached over their pen and gave their ears a good scratch each.

"Is this what you want? I have to go."

He propped his feet one at a time on the stoop to fasten his boots. Then tucking in his shirt as he walked, he rolled down his sleeves, and the dirt that had collected throughout the day fell free. He straightened his collar and vest and headed for the Montague villa wall. He brushed his hands through his brown mop of hair. It fell back where it had been, dancing around his warm eyes. His lips broke into a crooked smile at the thought of seeing Rosaline. He sped up.

Once he reached the wall, he grabbed a low-hanging branch and swung himself up into the tree. He climbed over the wall and jumped down.

The town of Verona was very much awake. The market was filled with merchants selling items they couldn't sell during the light of day to people who wouldn't be seen in town without the veil of night.

Benvolio ducked behind the church. Once he hit the cover of the sycamore grove, the air was cool on his face and almost damp compared to the dry dust of the town. The smell of the grove was always sweet. He looked up through the trees, and the moonlight hit the crooked branches. He took his time, stepping carefully over the jutting roots while ducking under the swooping limbs. Ahead of him, he could see their root. Rosaline wasn't there yet, so he planned to sit and wait for her, but a snap of a branch made him pause.

"Rosaline?" he whispered. He could hear her holding back her laughter. "Rose, don't you dare sneak up on me."

He felt her cool fingers through his shirt as she grabbed his arm and pulled him away from their root. "Where are we going?" he asked her.

"Just follow me," she said.

They ran through the trees. Then she let go of his hand and sprinted ahead of him. Her petticoat was covered in dirt.

"How long have you been in the woods, Rosaline?" Benvolio asked.

She just kept running. He was doing everything he could to keep up without falling or colliding into some part of a tree, but she kept looking back at him, making it difficult to concentrate.

She stopped. At her feet was a stream glistening black in the moonlight. The giant glaciers sitting heavily on the Alps had begun to melt, dripping down into the valleys of Verona.

"Wow, it's beautiful," Benvolio said as he looked at her. He sat down on a boulder and took off his boots. "Have you tested the water yet?"

"No," she said, smiling. "I've been waiting for you."

She sat on a root and took off her shoes. Grabbing the toes of her tights, she ripped a hole in them and hiked them up above her knees. Benvolio waited for her with his feet hovering over the water.

"Ready?"

"Ready," she said, smiling at him.

They slammed their feet into the stream.

"Oh, that's cold," Benvolio said.

"Keep them in until the back of your knees ache."

"I can't take it."

They pulled their feet out and let them rest in the warm, dry dirt lining the stream. Benvolio watched Rosaline as she leaned against the tree behind her and looked up into the stars. Every day had become about this moment for Benvolio. The moment he finally got to be alone in the woods with her. He looked at her in the moonlight and sat back against a rock. He saw she was wringing her hands anxiously in her lap.

"Rose?" he asked.

"Yes?" she said.

"Let me see your eyes."

She looked at him, widening her eyes as if they were being examined.

"They're blue," he said.

"Are they?" She looked back at the stars.

"How long have you been out here?"

"It was a beautiful day, Ben. Where else would I be?"

"What happened?"

"It was nothing." She turned to face him. "Do you remember Tybalt, my aunt's nephew?"

"I do."

"He's back in town."

"Does he still wear leather clothes and prance around like an angry cat?"

"Angry doesn't begin to explain Tybalt. He's filled with this need for a good fight. This morning at breakfast, I had to leave. He was getting my mother and my aunt all riled up against the Montagues. He doesn't know any more than we do what the fight is about. And still he sat there and spoke of revenge and getting even. My mother was excited at the idea of it all, and my aunt…well, I don't really understand what is going on with her. She began to act so strangely once Tybalt arrived. I had to get out of there."

"Have you been out here in the woods since breakfast?"

"I have."

"Are you starving?"

She smiled. "No, I found Romeo out here around dinnertime."

"Romeo was out here?"

"He was in the meadow, writing a poem. It's a very beautiful poem. I'm sure once he reads it to whomever it is he loves, she will fall madly in love with him, and he will stop being so melancholy."

"You think so?"

"I do. In fact, I was so sure he would recover easily that I had no problem taking some of his food."

"You took his food?" Benvolio said, laughing.

"He left it on a rock in the shade. He obviously wanted to share. Either I took it, or an animal would have."

"That's true."

"He had a napkin full of food and a bottle of wine. So I tore off some of the bread, grabbed a handful of fixings and a chunk of cheese, and went to the top of that boulder on the edge of the meadow and watched him all afternoon. I snuck back down and stole a sip or two of the wine, and he never even noticed me."

"I like that you spent the day with Romeo and that you were in some way there for each other."

They sat in silence, moving the water around with their feet and looking up at the stars. A cool breeze lifted Rosaline's hair and placed it on her shoulder. Without thinking, he brushed it off, feeling her silky curls against his rough hands. She didn't move away from his touch. He sat back against the rock.

"Does Romeo ever talk about the fight between our families?" she asked him.

"No, he never does. He just doesn't care about it. He's so full of passion and love. I don't think there's a place for this fight in his heart. Or maybe he's just so busy loving that he doesn't even notice what's happening around him."

"You're kind of the same way, Ben."

Emily Whitaker

"I am?"

"I mean, you're here with me."

He smiled at her.

"Anyway," she continued, "I was thinking what it would be like if this fight could die with our parents, but I know it can't. Tybalt is so angry. He could keep this fight alive all on his own. I'm afraid it will turn to death on both sides, and the deaths will fuel more rage. The cycle will continue until we all lose everything."

"Rosaline, that doesn't have to be what happens. Look at me. If Tybalt can fight this fight all by himself, then Romeo and you and I can stop it. If no one ever fights him, then Tybalt will look like a feral cat in heat, screaming all around town."

"As much as I would love to see that, you can't promise that you won't ever fight him back."

"I'll do what I can to keep the peace. I can at least promise you that."

"I believe you will."

Benvolio felt settled. He could handle Tybalt. He leaned back and closed his eyes, taking in the sweet scent of the orchard. His mind ran through thoughts of war to thoughts of food to where Romeo ran off to, and to who was hearing his poem at that very moment. The uneven sound of Rosaline's breath broke his trance and began to worry him.

"Rose?" he asked softly.

"There's more," she said.

Benvolio looked into her dark-blue eyes.

"My mother spoke to me this morning," she said. "She told me that my father is beginning to think of suitors for me to marry."

"He is what?" Benvolio said. "He's beginning to what?"

"My mother told me that it's time to get married. She said my uncle is doing the same with Juliet."

"But, Rose, I…what did you say to her?"

Rosaline smiled at Benvolio, and her breathing calmed. "You're getting upset."

"I am. Did she say whom your father was thinking of for suitors?"

"A few men in the prince's court."

"The prince's court?"

"Benvolio, what's wrong?" She was laughing.

"Rosaline, I…"

"What, Benvolio?"

"It can't be time for you to marry yet. I could tell your father stories about the men in the prince's court."

"Could you? And would you be present in these stories?"

"Listen, I mean, none of those men are good enough for you."

"Not good enough for me, a man on the prince's court? Well, then, I think you should tell my father everything. I mean, you have a strong opinion on the subject. Perhaps it would be good for my father to meet you as well."

"Do you think it would be?"

"Have you lost your mind, Benvolio?"

"Rose, I would do it. You said it yourself. I have no place in this fight. I would happily meet with your father, give him a strong handshake, and look him straight in the eye—"

"And say what? My name is Benvolio Montague?"

"Yes."

"My mother would have you removed before you could spit it out."

"Your mother doesn't scare me."

"Yes, she does, or at least she should, if you had any sense about you. Her hate for the Montagues is stronger than any others'. You know that. Even my uncle speaks of peace sometimes. It is a deeply rooted hate within her. A strong handshake can't break through it."

"It could."

"What are you saying, Benvolio? You would like to speak to my father about my hand in marriage?"

He cleared his throat and checked in with the gravel beneath his feet. Then he took a deep breath and looked up into her eyes. "Yes, I am, Rose. And why not? The Montagues are just as noble a family as the Capulets."

"Yes, they are." She smiled. "But noble doesn't win over one hundred years of hate for each other."

"Both of our families think that if we keep fighting, one of us will yield. In one hundred years, neither one of us has backed down. So why do we think continuing the fight, teaching us and our children and theirs to hate, is what we should keep doing? Do you know how kings would resolve a war like this one?" he asked.

"Conquer and pillage the land," she said.

"No," he said, a little frightened by her answer. "They would find peace by marrying the prince of one land to the princess of the other. I sit here before you tonight, Rosaline Capulet, and as a Montague, I yield in peace."

"You yield in peace to have my hand in marriage?"

"Yes," he said, feeling a bit dizzy

She smiled. "And you believe that shaking my father's hand could be the beginning of peace?"

"Rosaline, I do," he said as he stood. "I believe that love is the only thing strong enough to stop the hate our families have for each other."

"Love? Ben?"

His heart was pounding as he sat back against the rock. The warmth of Rosaline's hand was very near his, and he reached out for it. Her skin was soft to the touch. His hand was rough and hot, but she squeezed his hand and held it tight.

"Do you really believe that could work?" Rosaline whispered.

"I really do."

She didn't let go of his hand as they watched the stars move through the sky, and for the first time, Benvolio let himself think what the world would be like with peace between his family and hers. After all, he was holding her hand. He could find the strength to shake her father's.

"Rose, I'll shake your father's hand. I'll let your mother toss me out, and I'll return to shake his hand again and again and again."

Pulling his hand close to her, she turned and looked into his eyes; but before she could speak, she was interrupted by a startling call echoing through the grove.

"My lady Rosaline?" the call came through again.

"Nurse?" Rosaline yelled. "Benvolio, something must be wrong."

Benvolio pushed his wet feet back into his boots and turned to help her up, but she had already started running through the woods, her shoes in her hand. He chased after her.

"Nurse, I'm here," she yelled.

On Rosaline and Benvolio's usual meeting root, Rosaline's nurse was sitting, trying to catch her breath. They ran up to her.

"Are you all right?" Benvolio asked the nurse.

"Yes, I just need to catch my breath. Rosaline, it's your mother."

"Is she all right?" Rosaline asked.

"Yes. You had a gentleman come to visit you tonight."

"Oh no, one of the men my father's chosen?"

"Not exactly," the nurse said.

"Who was it?"

"It appears you have an admirer. The young Romeo Montague."

Rosaline looked to Benvolio, who was white in the face. "Please breathe, Ben. Nurse, did he have a poem to read to me?"

"He did," she answered.

"I should have known this would happen," Benvolio said. "Of course, he would fall in love with you. How could he not?" He was pacing behind Rosaline in the small space between the trees.

"Benvolio, please try to stay calm," Rosaline said. "We have to focus on what this means. A Montague walked into the Capulet villa to profess his love for me."

"Romeo loves you for one moment, and he has the courage to tell the world, to tell your mother. Oh God, your mother?" Benvolio said.

"Exactly, my mother. Now, Nurse, what happened when he read his poem?"

"I believe it was intended for your ears only, but your mother took it from him and read it aloud. It was quite good really, and the young Romeo did not change his tune no matter how hard she pushed him. He was determined to speak with you."

"My mother. Nurse, what did she do to him?"

"She called for you."

"Oh no," Rosaline said.

Emily Whitaker

"I answered for you. I told her you had gone to the chapel for prayer."

"Thank you, Nurse."

"Don't thank me yet, child. She knows."

"She knows?" Benvolio said, stopping his pacing to stand beside Rosaline.

"That incompetent twig, Gregory, your father's serving man, brought Romeo to your mother when he asked for you even though he should have turned him away. Anyhow, Gregory told your mother that you were not at the chapel. That you never go to the chapel, that you go to the woods to meet with a boy every night."

"Oh no, she knows everything," Rosaline said.

"He told her that you've been doing this for years now. Strange, really, how closely he has watched you. Your mother noticed his affection toward you as well. That didn't help matters."

"How will Lady Capulet react when you bring Rosaline home?" Benvolio asked.

"I suspect you will be punished, Rosaline, and that your father will push for a match to clear your good name."

"I can come with you to your mother," Benvolio said. "I can go to your father. Rosaline, let me try."

"You will do no such thing, young man," the nurse said as she stood. "Rosaline, your mother is involved and angered now. I believe the best thing for you is to come home with me, accept your punishment, and forget about these nights in the woods."

"But, Nurse—"

"I have let this go on for far too long. I only did so because I see how happy this time makes you. I saw all your pain go away each night, and you deserve to be happy, my sweet angel. So I let you have these nights in the woods with Benvolio, but now your punishment will be to make a life with a good man and raise your own children with the joy that lives in your heart."

"I can't marry some strange man, Nurse. You know I can't."

"I don't know that, and neither do you. Darling, there is nothing that can be done." She turned to Benvolio and took his hand. "You know her mother well, and tonight she is hot. Her temper is high, and it's not the right time for you. Do you understand me, young man? In these woods, it might not matter that you are a Montague, but the moment you enter those gates, it will matter very much. It mattered with your cousin, and he was not ousted for spending every night with young Rosaline in the woods. Believe me, Benvolio, this is for the best."

"But Rose—"

"Benvolio," the nurse said, stopping him. "Tonight I'll take care of Rosaline, as I have every time her mother is hot with anger. You can trust me, child. Trust me that tonight is not the night to fight her mother."

"I have no wish to fight her mother."

"Then you don't understand what it will take to become the man deserving of our Rosaline."

"But I do understand, and I don't think it will be a fight."

"Believe me, young man, tonight it will be. If you wish to keep the peace, then you will need to let the fire burn down. Rosaline, you will need to obey your parents' wishes, and you won't be able to return to these woods."

"She's right," Rosaline said. "Tonight is not the time, Benvolio." She leaned in and whispered, "But I'll meet you tomorrow, right here at our root. Come, Nurse."

Rosaline guided the nurse through the tricky grove. Benvolio followed them as they silently walked to the edge of the woods near the Capulet gates.

"You need to leave us here, son," the nurse said, continuing to walk out of the grove toward the Capulet villa.

Benvolio reached for Rosaline's hand once more, pulling her back into the cover of the trees. She smiled at him, squeezed his hand, and came closer to him. He could feel her breath on his chest. She looked into his eyes.

"Your eyes are brown," she said, smiling. "Like a cow's eyes after he eats a lot of grass."

He laughed. "Your eyes are still blue. It will be my life's mission to make them green again."

He slowly pulled her closer, listening to her breath, hearing that she wanted to be pulled toward him. He wrapped his arm around her waist. He could feel his heart beating strong and loud against hers. Her hand landed on his chest. It was cool and delicate against his hot skin.

"Rose, I—" he began.

"Rosaline." The nurse's voice startled them.

Rosaline softly laughed in his ear, sending goose bumps down his back. He held her closer.

"I'll see you tomorrow," she whispered, kissed him on the cheek, and turned away.

"Tomorrow," he said.

Benvolio watched Rosaline and the nurse enter the gates of the Capulet villa as he walked out of the woods toward the town. Slowly the gates creaked shut, and as they did, a figure came out from the moon's shade on the Capulet wall. With a heavy head, the figure was easily recognizable. It was Romeo, and he was walking toward the sycamore grove.

"Romeo?" Benvolio hollered.

Romeo stopped, turned, and looked at Benvolio; and without a word or gesture, he turned back and continued to walk away.

"You can have the solace of the woods, cousin," Benvolio whispered. "Tonight you were a stronger man than me."

Benvolio couldn't blame his cousin for falling in love with Rosaline. Benvolio had never told Romeo about his stolen nights with her in the woods or how he had loved her from the moment he first saw her. He knew that every time they passed Rosaline and her mother in the market, he would stop, and Romeo was always by his side. How could he think Romeo didn't see her beauty? He respected his cousin for his actions tonight. He knew it would take so much more than a beautiful poem to win the hand of their enemy's daughter, but at least tonight, Benvolio had taken a small step in that direction. He had told Rosaline his true feelings for her and held her. He never wanted to let her go.

Benvolio looked toward the Capulet villa. He felt sick at the thought of Rosaline inside, facing her mother's wrath. So he walked back into the woods and down the edge of the Capulet wall. With one hand grazing the face of the wall and the other hitting the low-hanging branches of the surrounding sycamores, he turned into the woods and jumped into a tree. He climbed a few branches and sat almost comfortably with his head resting on the thick trunk. It was the tree that reached over the wall for its mate. From there, he could see Rosaline's bedroom window. Fixing his eyes on the dark outline of the window, he waited for the flicker of candlelight to tell him that her mother had finished with her and she was safely in her room.

Benvolio found himself holding his breath. He had to trust that her nurse would do everything she could to protect and comfort Rosaline. His eyes stayed glued to her window as he kept time by the passing stars. The moon was disappearing and a bit of sun was filling in the east when he finally saw the candles light in her room.

Benvolio's heart lifted at the sight of it. He knew she was in pain, but now she could bury her head in her pillow.

And when the moon rose again in the sky, he would be in the woods waiting for her, ready to listen and maybe even hold her. The candlelight in Rosaline's room flickered and went out. She was settled in her bed, perhaps even peacefully asleep.

3

Jumping down from the tree, Benvolio walked back along the wall. The sun was hitting the town square, and the scene had changed greatly from the night. Servants and noblemen alike were turning up the dust as they passed by. Colorful fruits and salted meats were already on display. Benvolio rubbed his eyes and pushed his hands through his hair. He straightened his vest and collar, rolled up his sleeves, and headed into the crowded square. A red apple caught his eye, and he made his way to the cart.

"Good morning, Benvolio," the merchant said.

"Good morning. Just one, please," Benvolio said. He paid and followed his nose to a cart filled with steaming loaves of bread.

"I've got a sweet bun drizzled with honey and nuts just for you, Benvolio," the baker told him.

"I'll take it," Benvolio said as he held his apple in his mouth to pay the man.

With his breakfast in hand, he hopped up on the edge of the nearby fountain wall. Watching the people go about their day, he ate his apple and tried to enjoy his sweet bread. He had made a promise to find Romeo before his cousin could hide in his room and make him spend the day in the sun, but Benvolio couldn't stop thinking about Rosaline.

A flash of silver and the sound of clashing steel brought his mind back to the town square. He looked up. Through the crowd, he could see two men dressed in red and gold, his uncle's serving men. They had their swords drawn on two men in blue and green, Capulets. Benvolio tossed his apple core and sweet bread and reached for his sword. Pushing his way through the crowd to the men, he brought down their swords with a swift blow.

"Enough," he yelled. "You fools! Put your swords away. Do you have any idea what these fights between us mean? Or the amount of trouble they cause?" Benvolio took their silence to mean they had settled down. He stepped back to put his sword away, but behind him came a familiar voice full of scratch and whine.

"Benvolio," Tybalt said. "Your sword is drawn among my men." Tybalt circled Benvolio like he was prey. "Are you threatening my servants? What a weak move. And why am I surprised? This is an obvious move from a Montague. I don't suppose you're man enough to fight me?"

Standing in front of Benvolio, Tybalt slowly pulled his sword from its sheath and examined the slick blade. The black leather sheath descended along his tight pant leg; the silver and shiny jewels lining it matched those on his boots. His dark hair was tight against his head with grease, and not one hair was out of place. His lips snarled into a wicked smile.

"You understand the difference between a fair fight of two trained noblemen as opposed to attacking my ignorant servants?" Tybalt said. "Or are you just afraid I'll kill you?" Tybalt's laugh ripped like a wild scream, and a low purr came from his gut as he fixed his yellow eyes on Benvolio.

"Tybalt," Benvolio said softly, with his sword at his side, pointing down. "I drew my sword to keep the peace between these men. That is all. Please, only raise your sword beside me if it's to help me stop these men from fighting."

"Don't tell me you believe drawing your sword can bring peace among men?" Tybalt stepped toward Benvolio. "Because if you believe it's the Montagues who are acting in peace, then it's peace that I hate. I hate it as much as I hate hell. As much as I hate all Montagues, Benvolio. As much as I hate you." Tybalt lunged toward Benvolio with his sword.

Benvolio blocked his blow reactively with his sword and fell to one knee. With all his might, he held Tybalt's sword above his head. Tybalt swung his sword behind him, aiming for Benvolio's open side; but Benvolio rolled behind Tybalt and, with the grip of his sword, buckled Tybalt's knees and stood as Tybalt fell. Springing to his feet, Tybalt turned and, with the tip of his sword, lunged toward Benvolio's heart. Benvolio stepped to the side as Tybalt's blade sliced into his arm.

"Citizens of Verona, enough!" the booming voice of Escalus, the prince of Verona, demanded.

Benvolio's sword fell to his side, as did Tybalt's. The silence rang in Benvolio's ears as he looked through the crowd that had formed to watch them fight. He put his head down as he knelt beside his sword. He could see Rosaline's face in his mind, her tired eyes, and tearstained cheeks from a night of fighting for him. And how did he honor her? By raising his sword at Tybalt the first time Tybalt challenged his peaceful resolve.

The prince began to speak, "Another brawl between the houses of Montague and Capulet." The prince addressed the crowd while circling Benvolio and Tybalt. "Are you aware that we men of Verona only arm ourselves to keep the people safe from your families? You Montagues and Capulets bring disgrace to us all when you draw your weapons to harm one another. We speak to you like men. We speak to you like citizens, like neighbors. But you never listen to us."

The prince jumped on the ledge of a flowing fountain and looked over the crowd. "You men have become beasts. Your rage is painting our city with blood, and we will not stand for it any longer. Throw down your weapons and hear the sentence of your angry prince. If you ever disturb the quiet of our streets again, you will pay with your life. For now, everyone needs to go their separate ways. You, Capulet, will come with me. Montague, you will meet me at Old Freetown court of law this afternoon to know your punishment in this mess."

Benvolio looked up. He didn't know his uncle was there and had seen him fighting. He stood and dusted off the dirt on his knees. Then he faced his uncle. He dropped his gaze back to the ground when he saw his aunt standing with him. She looked tired with worry. Her hair was gray and fell gracefully from her bun. Dark circles had taken over her eyes. She was holding on to her husband for a bit of support.

"Who started this wicked fight again?" Lord Montague asked Benvolio. "Please, tell me, Ben. Were you here when it began?"

"I was," Benvolio said as he grabbed his bleeding arm. "Your servants and the serving men of the house of Capulet began to fight. I noticed it from across the town square. Uncle, I only drew my sword to keep the peace between them, I swear, but Tybalt came, and you know how angry he is. He's always looking for a fight. I tried to tell him that I was only keeping the peace, but he didn't believe me. He didn't want to believe me. He came to town this morning wanting to fight. He swung his sword at me, and I blocked it. He continued to fight me, and I kept defending myself. I didn't realize the people of Verona were watching us. I was only trying to stop him, Uncle. And that's when the prince came."

"And Romeo?" Lady Montague asked, her voice shaking. "I'm grateful he isn't here in this fight, but, Benvolio, have you seen him today? He wasn't at home this morning."

"Madam, I did see him this morning, before the sun came up. I was out because I couldn't sleep last night, and I find it comforting to walk through the town. And anyway, I saw Romeo in the sycamore grove west of the city. I wanted to join him, but when he saw me, he hid in the trees and walked away from me. I understood he wanted solitude, so I let him be alone. I think that was what he wanted."

Lord Montague stood tall, his large belly pushing at his vest buttons. His cheeks were flushed with the excitement of the fight, but his eyes were focused with worry. He looked into the crowd.

"I've heard that Romeo walks in the sycamore grove all night and into the early morning," he said. "I hear that his face is wet with tears. His heart is as heavy as the clouds are gray. Benvolio, listen to me. Romeo might be turning away from everyone, but I truly believe he has never needed anyone as much as he does now. I need you to talk to my son, and I need you to try this time, even if he walks away from you again."

"Uncle, do you know why he's acting this way?" Benvolio asked.

"I don't know, and I can't find out from him why he is acting this way. He won't talk to me."

"You've tried talking to him?"

"I have. I have tried. I've sent in many friends as well, but he won't talk to anyone. He consoles himself, I suppose, but to be alone in your darkness makes you so far away from reason and truth. He needs to turn to someone. I've never seen him turn away from you. It worries me that he hasn't spoken to you about this yet. It's important that you push him to talk to you. If I can understand what started this, I will do whatever it takes to cure it."

"You would do whatever it takes?" Benvolio asked with a deep breath. He wanted to ask him, if his son were in love with a Capulet, would he be willing to yield in peace to the Capulets to help him? "Look, there's Romeo. Uncle, I'll go and talk to him. Both of you can return to your day and let us talk. I promise I'll find out what's troubling Romeo, and we can stop all this."

"I want to stay. I want to understand my son," Lord Montague said with a heavy sigh and a soft touch from his wife. "But no, you're right. You will have better luck without us around. Come, madam." Lord Montague took the hand of his wife. "Let's get back to our day."

Benvolio turned from his uncle toward Romeo. He rolled up his sleeves to hide the gash on his arm and brushed his hands through his hair. His brown locks fell back into his eyes.

Romeo was leaning against a wall at the bottom of a few steps.

"Good morning, Romeo," Benvolio said.

"Oh, is it still only morning?" Romeo mumbled.

His head was hanging, and his hair was somehow perfectly falling to hide his brooding eyes. Though he had been in the woods all night, his shirt fell perfectly crisp around his broad shoulders. His face was soft, not shining with the heat of the morning sun.

"Yes, it's only nine o'clock," Benvolio said.

Romeo sighed heavily. "Every depressing hour creeps by so slowly. Was that my father that just left?"

"Yes, Romeo. He's worried about you, and so am I. What's so depressing that it makes today creep by so slowly?"

"Not having that which makes time fly."

Benvolio took a seat on the step beside Romeo. "Are you in love?" Benvolio asked him.

"Out—"

"Of love?" he asked again.

"You wouldn't understand."

"Give me a chance."

Romeo began to walk away. "It's just that the woman I love, the woman who has stolen my heart, is not mine to have."

"I actually do understand that, Romeo. I do," Benvolio said, running to catch up to Romeo. "You mean you're able to see and know of her beauty, but there are obstacles that stop you from ever truly being with her? I do know how painful that can be."

"Yes, that's the kind of love I'm talking about. Love that has never been given the chance to be seen clearly or given time to find a path to make it work."

The summer's heat was beginning to beat down on them. Romeo lay in the cool mist of a fountain.

"I'm hungry, where do you want to eat?" Romeo asked as he lazily turned his head and looked at Benvolio for the first time. "Stop." He leapt to his feet and grabbed Benvolio's arm that had bled through his shirt. "What's this, Benvolio? Were you in a fight? No, I don't want to hear it. I've heard it all before. You all think this fight has to do with hate, but you don't understand how much it has to do with love. Why then? Why would you fight love, and how can you love to hate each other? Or what, Benvolio, because I don't get it. What was it that came first? You say you understand the love that's in my heart, and still you draw your sword."

"To keep the peace," Benvolio said.

"You fight to keep the peace? Do you kill to live? Do we all fight this fight for good reasons? Is there ever a good reason to fight? A hateful reason to love? Is there such a thing as well-placed chaos or a feather of lead, bright smoke, cold fire, sick health? You ask me what my problem is. Well, what am I supposed to make of this?" he said, grabbing Benvolio's arm. "What am I supposed to make of this love that I feel if nothing around me makes any sense? Is there no love to feel then?"

Benvolio sighed.

"What?" Romeo asked. "Are you laughing at me?"

"No, it was a sigh. Romeo, if anything, I'm crying for you."

"Fine. If you're crying for me, then tell me why."

"I'm crying at the pain you're feeling. You do understand all the chaos that's around you. I think you're the only one who can make sense of it all."

"Why would you laugh or cry at my pain when my pain is full of love? I'm in love, and this pain is what love is. It's my pain to feel, and now I have to add to it because of your act of violence. Why? Because I'm the only one who understands it. Now I have to feel your pain because I love you, and I'll take that burden. At least until you can truly understand what it means to feel love. Then you might understand why you should stop fighting. Because love is smoke made with the fume of sighs," Romeo said, putting his arm around Benvolio. "When that love is truly expressed, it's a fire sparkling in lovers' eyes. When a lover is angered, it's a sea filled with tears. I have to go." He turned and walked away.

"Wait," Benvolio said, following him. "I'll go with you. You can't just leave me like this."

"I have to. I'm not myself now."

"You have to tell me, Romeo, who is it whom you love so much? What has happened to you that makes your love so painful? You can talk to me."

"What, you want me to start to cry again just so I can tell you her name? Because that's what it will cost me."

"No more crying. Just talk to me, please. Come on, tell me her name," Benvolio said, chasing Romeo through the crowded streets.

"I'm a sick man in this sadness I call love. Every word I speak about this love is ill because of it, so in my sadness, I'll tell you. I do love a woman."

"A woman, no way!" Benvolio said sarcastically as he grabbed Romeo's arm and stopped him from walking away. "I would have guessed as much."

"Oh, well, good guess then. Ah, she's a beautiful woman."

"Okay, beautiful is good, so what is making you so sad about her? Tell me what happened. Tell me her name."

"In her case, it's her beauty that will keep her from love."

"It's her beauty that will keep her from love?"

"She has Dian's wit, and because of that, she will live chaste."

"She has what? Wait, she will live chaste? What makes you say that?"

"Throughout her life, she will remain untouched by love's spells. She won't be the object of man's affection, and she will never be allowed to enjoy their attentions upon her. She will never know the feel of a lover's touch."

"I know what *chaste* means, Romeo. But why do you think your love will be living chaste?"

"Oh, she is so rich in beauty, yet poor, because when she dies, her beauty won't live on in the face of her children. She has sworn to live chaste, and with that vow, she is wasting all that God has blessed her with. Her beauty will starve without my love."

"So you are sad because you realized you were chasing the love and affection of someone who is going to promise herself to God?" Benvolio couldn't figure out whom Romeo was talking about now. Could Rosaline's part in the drama of the night been confused? But he knew of no woman in the Capulet villa who was sworn to live chaste.

"She is too beautiful and yet too wise," Romeo said. "She has turned her back on love, and with that vow, I die. Benvolio, I'm a dead man talking to you now."

"Romeo, listen to me. You need to forget about this woman, whoever she is. Who is she?"

"Teach me how I should forget to think at all because she is my every thought."

"I'll teach you. Open your eyes and look around at all the beautiful women of Verona. You can't have this love of yours, but you can have her," Benvolio said, pointing out a woman. "Or her. She is very, um, nice-looking?"

"This isn't working, Benvolio. With every passing face, I'm only reminded of her beauty. There's no hope for me. Soon my love will hide her brow in a black veil and promise herself to God. Oh, you could blind me, and I would still see her and only her. There is none as glorious or as pure as my love. Maybe you can show me another beautiful woman, but with every face you show me, I can show you another man who has touched that beautiful woman. So goodbye. I would never want to forget my love, and you can't teach me how." Romeo started to walk quickly through the crowded streets.

"I'll take that as a challenge, Romeo. I'll teach you, or I'll die trying," Benvolio said, running to keep up with him. He had to figure out Rosaline's part in this. He needed to know everything so he could help Romeo—and Rosaline.

"How will you teach me?" Romeo asked.

"First, tell me more about your love."

"I have told you everything."

"You've told me about her beautiful face. Tell me about her soul, what you do to make her laugh, her favorite food. Tell me why you love her so deeply. Tell me her name."

"You're talking like a lover, Benvolio."

"Am I? That's interesting. What is her name?"

"I can't say it because it's her name that has given her this dreadful fate."

"Her name is why she's becoming a nun?"

"A name can be very powerful when the name is that of your enemy."

"So she is a Capulet? Romeo, tell me what her name is."

"A Capulet, yes. I don't care about this fight between our families. How can I, when love is always more powerful than hate?"

"I agree with you, but this is very important. You're telling me that you are in love with a Capulet, and it's her will to become a nun? I need you to tell me who she is."

"What I'm telling you, Benvolio, is that because she is blessed with such beauty, it's decided that the safest place for her to live is the nunnery. Only there can she live without the eyes and hands of the many men who desire her."

"The woman you love has chosen to become a nun because she doesn't enjoy getting attention from men?"

"I'm telling you that upon hearing word of my love for her daughter, as well as a stranger's love in the woods and, I'm guessing, the serving man's love for her, Lady Capulet banished her daughter, Rosaline, to a nunnery."

Benvolio froze. He needed to get to Rosaline for answers. He turned to Romeo and realized he couldn't afford to be selfish yet.

"Romeo, listen to me." Benvolio said. He started walking, and Romeo followed. "Your love for Rosaline will burn out, and before you know it, another fire within you will burn with passion for a different beautiful woman. I promise you. The pain you're feeling now will lessen when you find this new love."

"Benvolio?" Romeo stopped him.

"Yes?"

"This isn't helping."

"Right. Look, I just want you to be happy, and by turning this around, your grief can be cured by loving someone else."

"I really don't think that will do it."

"Just fall in love with someone else, and I promise the pain of this love will all fade away."

"This sounds more like a bandage, not a cure for my pain."

"A bandage, Romeo, really? Is your heart that broken?"

"Your shins will be soon if you keep trying to make me forget my love."

Benvolio realized he was pushing too hard. He stopped and looked up. Without meaning to, they had both made turns through town that led them to the gates of the Capulet villa. The gates stood open to make way for the business of the day. Benvolio stared at them.

He wanted to run to Rosaline. He wanted to scream about the news of the nunnery. He wanted to shake her father's hand and slap her mother. But he was already on the list of men forcing her into the nunnery. He needed to take care of Romeo before he could find a way to get to Rosaline. But he knew he couldn't wait until she met him in the woods tonight to ask her about something this huge. He realized there was nothing he could do at that moment and turned to Romeo, who was sad once again at the sight of the gates.

"Romeo," Benvolio said, playfully starting back in. "Have you gone mad?"

"Not mad, but tied up tighter than a madman. I'm shut up in prison, kept without food, whipped and tormented and—good afternoon, good fellow," Romeo said to the odd serving man who had walked up to them.

"God gives you this good evening," he said. "Can you read, sir?" he asked Romeo.

"Yes, I'm fortunate enough to be terrible at it," Romeo answered.

"All right, sir. Maybe you've learned to read without a book, but I beg you, can you read anything you see?"

"Sure, if I know the letters and the language."

"I get it. Thank you anyway."

"Stay, fellow, I can read."

The serving man handed Romeo a letter. He took the letter from the man and began to read name after name of the most pompous and arrogant citizens of Verona. Benvolio lost interest and looked back to the Capulet gates, and there she was.

Standing in the glow of the sun was Rosaline. She was looking right at him with her playful smile. Her hair was shining gold in the sunlight. Her skin glowed, and her cheeks were rosy. Her dress looked odd; it was plain black without the shimmer of blue or green. Benvolio stepped toward her, but she stopped him with a look to her mother. How could he miss her mother standing beside her, trying to be her double, only lacking greatly in beauty, and making up for it with her fancy, shiny dress? Surrounding her mother was a circle of ladies all hanging on her every word, laughing as if she were wonderful. Rosaline turned back to Benvolio. She smiled at him and pointed behind him. He looked back and then back to her. He didn't understand. She pointed again and then moved her hands and eyes like she was reading a list. She smiled, and he could see she was laughing at him. Once more she pointed to Romeo, pretended she was reading a list of names, pointed to her ears, then brushed him away toward Romeo. He turned back to Romeo, who was still reading the list, and finally Benvolio understood.

"Signor Placentio and his lovely nieces," Romeo was saying. "Mercutio and his brother, Valentine."

"Mercutio?" Benvolio interrupted. "What is this list for?"

Romeo shrugged in confusion and continued to read. "My uncle Capulet, his wife, and daughters. My fair niece, Rosaline and Livia."

Romeo looked to Benvolio, who again froze. He couldn't let Romeo see him look back at Rosaline.

"Interesting, keep reading," Benvolio said.

Romeo kept reading. Benvolio looked back to Rosaline, but she was gone, and so was her mother.

Romeo finished reading and handed the list back to the serving man "This is a fine list of people. Where are they supposed to meet?"

"Up," answered the serving man.

"Right, but where? Why? For supper?"

Benvolio

"To our house."

"Whose house?"

"My master's."

"Indeed, I should have asked you that first."

"Well, now, I'll just tell you. My master is the great and rich Lord Capulet, and as long as you are not a Montague, you should come to the party and have a cup of wine. I have to go. Have a great day."

He bowed and walked away.

"Rosaline will be at this party," Benvolio said. "I mean, we should go to this party because Rosaline will be there, and then I'll be able to show you beauties that are far better than her in comparison. I promise you will realize she is not so great." He looked around to make sure she wasn't there to hear him.

"My eyes will never see another woman. I'm devoted to my love for Rosaline. If my eyes betray me as you say they will, I hope they burn out. I mean, come on, Benvolio, have you seen my love? To show me anyone that's more beautiful than her is impossible. Please, you make me laugh. Never on this earth has a woman walked that's more beautiful than Rosaline."

He couldn't agree more. "Come on, Romeo," he said. "You say she's beautiful, but what are you comparing her to? She's probably beautiful if all you see is her, looking at her through eyes that haven't begun to see the beauty of the world. So all I ask is that you come with me to this party tonight and compare her beauty to those I show you. Even though she seems like the only beauty in the world, she's not."

"I'll go with you, but I'll see no other beauties. I'll go only for the chance to be in the presence of Rosaline one more time."

"Right. Well, come on then. We have to find Mercutio if we want to get into this party."

4

The dust from the streets in town reflected blue in the moonlight. Mercutio told them to meet him by the Fountain of Fairies after sunset. When they arrived, Mercutio was lying on the edge of the fountain, staring at the sky. He was playing with a sharp knife in his hand. It was encrusted with red and blue jewels, which sparkled as he tossed it about. His boots flopped carelessly around his ankles, unlaced. And his shirt, though it was tucked in, sat open on his chest. He propped himself up on one elbow and looked at Benvolio and Romeo. His blond hair was long, and the curls fell around his eyes. He smiled his mischievous smile and handed them their masks.

"I don't feel right about this," Romeo said as he put on his mask. "What do we say when we get there? How do we explain why we came to their party? Or do we just go and not apologize for it? Like we have no care in the world?"

"Romeo, we don't need to explain ourselves," Benvolio said. "It's a masquerade. They won't know who we are. Besides, who explains why they're dancing when they could just dance?" Benvolio was about to see Rosaline. He was excited. He couldn't hide it. "We'll go to their party, and who cares what they think of us? Who cares what we think about them? We will scout out their beautiful women, have a dance or two, drink their wine, and leave."

"Well, then, at least let me carry the torch. I'm not in the mood for a party or dancing. My heart is heavy, so I should be burdened with the weight of the light."

"Oh, come on, Romeo," Mercutio said, leaping off the fountain and dancing toward him. "Don't be so sad. You have to dance."

"No," Romeo said. "Don't you see? You have dancing shoes with nimble soles. My soul is heavy in my pain and, like lead, holds me to the ground. I won't dance."

"I thought you were a lover, Romeo," Mercutio said.

"Is that what I am?" Romeo asked.

"Yes, you are, so borrow Cupid's wings to dance tonight."

"I can't. It's Cupid who has stabbed me in the heart. His light feathers couldn't lift me from the heavy weight of lost love."

"You're making love sound like a terrible thing, Romeo."

"Do you think love is a tender thing, Mercutio? Oh no, it's rough. It's mean and full of trickery and will prick you like a thorn. As if getting stung with Cupid's poisoned arrow wouldn't hurt."

"Now I'm interested. A love that pricks? Prick it back, I say. Believe me, that will ease all this pain you feel."

"It's not that kind of love I'm talking about."

"Perhaps it should be. Every woman tonight will be wearing a mask, but how is that different from how they are every moment of every day? It's not, so I say, don't take the time to care who you find tonight. Just find a woman of any kind and prick out this pain you feel."

"Great, glad we have a plan. Now let's go," Benvolio said.

"I'll go," Romeo said. "But please let me carry the torch. I don't feel like dancing."

"Still with the torch?" Mercutio said. "Fine, let's go. We're wasting the daylight trying to make you dance."

"It's night," Romeo said.

"I know what time of day it is. I mean we are wasting life as we sit here fighting to bring up your spirits."

"Should we even go then?"

"Oh, come on, Romeo," Benvolio said. "Let's just go and see what it's like."

"I mean, are we even going for the right reason? I really don't think we are," Romeo said, as if Benvolio weren't even talking.

"And why do you think we shouldn't go?" Mercutio said.

"Well, I had a dream tonight," Romeo said.

"Well, so did I," Mercutio countered.

"Oh, you did? And what was your dream about?"
"That dreamers often lie."
"I was lying down while I had my dream about truth."
"Oh, so Queen Mab has been with you as you sleep?"
"Who?"
"She is a small fairy," Mercutio said as he leapt back onto the fountain.

"And here he goes," Benvolio said, defeated.

"She is no bigger than a small jewel set upon your finger," Mercutio continued. "Her carriage is drawn by creatures as tiny as atoms. As men sleep, she flies over their noses in her chariot." He began to dance along the edge of the fountain. "Oh, her chariot, it is something wild. The spokes are made of spider legs. The cover is made of grasshopper wings. She is strapped in by the smallest spiderweb and beams of the moon's light. Her whip is made of crickets' bones and fine thread. The driver of her chariot is a small gray gnat. The body of her chariot is a hollowed-out hazelnut, made for her by a cabinet-making squirrel. Or perhaps simply just a grubworm who ate it out."

Mercutio laughed and knelt down to meet Romeo's face. "You see, moments into your sleep after your mind has drifted, she visits you. She does this night after night. She visits lovers' brains and lets them dream of their love." He messed up Romeo's hair and pushed him out of his way as he leapt down to meet face-to-face with a stranger passing by. "She visits the knees of the lords and ladies of the king's court, and immediately they dream of kneeling low, bowing, and curtsying before their king."

The passerby walked away quickly. Mercutio turned to Benvolio and grabbed his hand. "She visits the fingers of lawyers, who immediately dream of money and fees." Mercutio turned back to Romeo. "She passes over the lips of ladies, who quickly dream of kisses. But this sometimes angers Queen Mab, so she plagues these women with blisters on their lips. But what is it about this that angers her?"

He moved close to Romeo's face. "It's their breath as she flies over their lips. It's artificially sweetened with candy." He turned and jumped back onto the fountain. "And this fills her with rage. And sometimes she will fly over the noses of a lord of the king's court, and he will dream of the opportunity to present a case to the king on someone's behalf. And sometimes she will tickle the nose of a man with the tail of a pig he gave to the church as his tithe, and he will dream of giving more. Sometimes she will drive her chariot over the neck of a soldier, and he will dream of killing his enemies by slitting their throats. Their dreams will flood with forts they have built to hide inside."

Mercutio stepped into the water of the fountain and walked to the fairies in the center. "They will dream of ambushes, their enemies attacking them from behind again and again, from every side as they sit unprepared, stunned, bloody." He ran his hands along the sculptures. "Spanish blades made of Toledo steel slicing through the air about them, slicing through them, slicing. And then immediately she will have drums play in their ears, forcing them to wake with a start." He slowly sank into the water, his cheeks against the cool marble. He wrapped his hands around a fairy's waist. "Frightened in his bed, the soldier will pray for peace and sleep again."

Mercutio sat silent. He stared at the water as it fell around him. He followed the drops up toward the sky, and a smile broke across his face. "Oh yes, this is the same Queen Mab that braids horses' manes at night and tangles the hair of women who spend their nights in bed on their backs. And with this, she angers even the elves who must untangle this woman's unfortunate body. But in this fight with the elves, Queen Mab will always win, keeping women on their backs so they may learn to bear the act that will make them women."

"Oh, calm down, Mercutio," Romeo said. "Get out of the fountain. What are you even talking about?"

"Yes, Romeo, it's nonsense I speak because I speak of dreams," Mercutio said as he stood and casually walked out of the fountain. "Dreams are the creation of a sleeping mind. They mean nothing and are only your fantasies, and fantasies are worthless. They are nothing. You can't grab them as you can't grab the air. They are inconsistent, coming and going like the wind. The wind that's now coming from the cold north but by morning will be so angered, it will pout away from us, and as it turns its back, it will be pushed by the breeze of the south, who will greet us with dewdrops."

Benvolio stepped in. "This wind you're talking about sounds like a lot of hot air. Supper is over. Come on, already. It's time for us to crash this masquerade."

"It isn't me that you need to convince," Mercutio said as he turned to walk to the party, leaving wet footsteps behind.

"Are you sure we won't be too early?" Romeo asked.

Without answering, Benvolio turned to follow Mercutio.

"I just don't feel right about this," Romeo yelled as he ran to catch up. "We are going into the house of our enemy. Even if we don't get caught, I feel like the consequences of our actions tonight will play out in time as a wicked tragedy."

"What a dreadful thought," Benvolio said, putting his arm around Romeo. "We're on our way to a party."

"You're right. Fine, forget this feeling. If you want to guide me to whatever may happen tonight, I'll let you. Direct me, Benvolio. Come on."

"Yes, let's go," Benvolio said as he pushed Romeo toward the Capulet gates.

5

Benvolio had only known the Capulet villa as the stone towers that stood tall enough to see over the wall surrounding their land and what he could see from atop the trees. He was excited to truly see the villa for the first time, though he wished the circumstances were much different. As the gates opened, Benvolio felt heavy on his feet and nervous. He made sure his mask covered his face and hoped his mop of hair wouldn't give him away.

"Welcome to the Capulet villa," said the guard standing watch at the gate.

When they made it through the gate, Benvolio looked at Rosaline's home for the first time. Before him was a straight path of pure white stone heading to the villa's main entrance. Lining the path were perfectly round bushes spaced uniformly, and beyond them stood tall trimmed trees. The grass was evenly cut, and the yard went on forever. Large boulders were placed on the lawn in alignment.

Benvolio wondered if there was anything natural about their land and realized why Rosaline had to escape to the woods to be her true self.

The steps of the villa led to two large wooden doors. Standing small in their shadow was another guard allowing the guests to enter the home. Benvolio secured his mask again and followed Mercutio. Romeo was still dragging behind them.

They followed the crowd to the main hall. The inside of the Capulet villa was even more of a show than the outside. Everything was covered in gold. Enormous crystal chandeliers hung one after the other, lining the pathway from the grand entrance to the main hall. The walls were busy with portraits, and the floors were cold, hard marble. When they entered the main hall, Lord Capulet, Rosaline's uncle, was speaking to his guests.

"Yes, you are all welcome, gentlemen. Musicians, let's hear some music."

The hall burst with excitement as the music began.

"Benvolio," Romeo yelled. "I don't think we should stay."

"Come on, Romeo, enough. We've been welcomed, and there's dancing, which means there are women," Benvolio said as he searched the crowd for Rosaline.

"I'm not sure what to do with myself," Romeo said.

"We'll follow Mercutio. He was actually invited, so I'm sure he feels welcome. Come on. He went this way toward the music."

"I know this song," Romeo said with a smile.

"Then come, let's dance," Benvolio said.

They stepped into the dance floor, exchanging partners step by step. Benvolio watched Romeo's face until he saw his despair change to wonderment. Benvolio knew that look well; it was the look of a man who had a beautiful woman in his sights. Within moments, Romeo disappeared in pursuit of that beautiful woman, leaving Benvolio free to find Rosaline.

Beyond the dance floor was a staircase leading to a terrace that wrapped around the edge of the main hall. Benvolio ran up the stairs for a better view of the crowd. He leaned over the golden rail and saw many young women with their dark hair pulled up and masks hiding their faces. Scanning every one of them, he began to walk the edge of the terrace. He watched them dance and could tell it was not how Rosaline moved. He watched them laugh and knew that was not how Rosaline laughed. After making a complete loop along the terrace, he looked behind him.

Drapes hung along the wall, and from behind the drapes, Benvolio could hear people's voices. He peered between an opening in the fabric, and he could see velvet couches wrapped around tables with drinks and wild foods. Rosaline wouldn't be inside one of the private booths. She knew he was coming; she would help him find her. But he knew her mother would hide her, especially if she were going to join the nunnery in a day. Benvolio desperately peered through every opening in the fabric he could find. He opened his ears, knowing she would speak loudly to help him find her, and immediately he heard her voice. He fixed his mask and quickly brushed his hands through his hair, then opened the drapery. His eyes closed, and he quickly shut the drapery. That was not Rosaline. He heard her voice again and followed it.

"Speak once more, Rosaline," he whispered.

"I will do that," he heard her say loudly.

He found her and stepped toward her. He tried not to think that her mother was most likely sitting next to her. He opened the drapery. His eyes locked on to hers, and suddenly he could not speak. She was in her simple, plain black dress. She wore no mask. Her hair was down, sitting naturally on her shoulders, and she was as beautiful as ever. Benvolio could see that her eyes were red around the edges from tears, but she smiled brightly at him. He put his hand out to her, and she looked to the seat across from her. Sitting silently was Sister Mary Margaret, dressed in black cloth and a white cap. She smiled at Benvolio, the familiar smile she'd given him at church. He paused.

"Good evening," Sister Mary Margaret said to him.

"Good evening, Sister," he replied and cleared his throat.

"I presume you are here to ask our sweet Rosaline for a dance?"

"I am."

Emily Whitaker

"I believe I hear her mother calling for me. I must go keep her company." She stood and whispered to Benvolio, "Do not speak with her here, my son. Take her into the crowd." She put something into his hand and walked away.

Benvolio looked down and saw a feathery mask.

"Rosaline," he said.

Rosaline was pulling her hair back, and she wrapped it into a messy bun. "May I have that mask, please?" she asked him.

He handed it to her and watched as she transformed herself to blend into the party. With a smile, she stepped out of the private area and closed the drapery behind her to make it look like it was still occupied. She took his hand and rushed him down the stairs into the crowd on the dance floor.

Along the walls of the hall stood tall tapestries hanging from golden rods. Rosaline led him to the wall and took a quick look around. Then she grabbed the edge of a tapestry and pulled Benvolio into a small cold crevice behind it. It was quiet and calm.

"I told you I would see you tonight," she said.

"You did say that," he said.

"You're sad, Ben."

"You're really going to become a nun?"

"I'll be joining the nunnery tomorrow morning. My mother said that it's time for me to marry, and if I won't marry one of the men my father has chosen, then this is my only option. And if I'm only attracting the attention of Montagues, serving men, and strangers that force me into the woods, then I'm not suitable to be introduced into society as a pure young woman ripe for marriage."

"Ripe?"

"Her word, not mine."

"What can I do?"

"What do you mean?"

"This nunnery is just another cage, Rose."

She smiled. "I'm going to miss you calling me Rose."

"Look at me." He took her face in his hands. Her cheek rested against his large hand so delicately. "Why are you going along with this?"

"What choice do I have?"

"Me, you could choose me."

"Oh, Ben," she said. Falling into him, she put her head on his broad shoulder and began to cry.

"Please look at me." He pulled her from his shoulder and looked into her watery blue eyes. "I want to marry you, Rose. I'll go to your mother and say it to her face. I'll tell her that you are ripe for marriage, and I'm the man to pluck you."

She laughed. "Please don't ever say that."

"I won't say that, but, Rose, I don't want you to join the nunnery."

"I need you to try to see this from my point of view. Do you see what my alternative is?"

"To not become a nun."

"No." She smiled. "I'm ripe for marriage, it's true. And that means that if it's not the nunnery, it's a man. And I learned last night from my mother and my father's reaction to Romeo's poem and confession of love that it cannot be a Montague. That it will be a man that I don't love. And if I can't marry the man that I do love, then I can't marry anyone. And I'll never be allowed to marry you."

He grabbed her hands and held them tight to his chest. He leaned toward her. He smelled her sweet breath and wrapped his arm tightly around her waist. Lifting her up to him, he met her lips with his. He kissed her, holding her as tightly to him as he could. She kissed him back, removing his mask and tangling her fingers in his hair. Their tears met on their cheeks and fell to their lips. She let out a little laugh and tried to bury her face in his chest. He lifted her chin gently to look into her eyes.

"Your eyes are green," he told her.

She smiled.

"I could go to your mother now," he said. "And to your father and announce my love for you. I'll tell them that I want to marry you. I may be a Montague, but that name is still rich. I could do it now in front of all of these people. The prince has men here. Maybe they will tell him about my offer of peace and force your parents to accept. Besides, what do you have to lose now? Your mother can't kill me in front of all these people."

"Yes, she can. No matter how much you swear your love for me, they will never see past your name. They won't forget that you were the man who pulled his sword on our men today and fought with Tybalt."

"You heard about that?"

"I did."

"I'm so sorry, Rosaline. After last night, after what you had gone through, I told you I wouldn't fight."

"And I told you it would be impossible to keep that kind of promise."

"Would you believe me if I told you it was to keep the peace?"

"I would have also believed self-defense," she said.

"So you're not mad?"

"Ben, it proves that my decision is the only answer. Our families will always fight. If this is a world where a man like you finds the need to raise his sword, then it's not a world where we can openly love each other. As long as I'm a Capulet and you are a Montague—"

"Then I'll stop being a Montague."

"Then you won't be a suitable match for me. You will have no home, no job, no money, and no future."

"Wow, I knew my name had power, but I never realized how much it defined who I am."

"I have thought of every option, Ben, believe me."

"You've thought about every option of how we could spend the rest of our lives together?"

"I have."

He held her close to him. Her hair smelled like the sycamore grove.

"We could run," he said. "We could go live in Mantua. I know we'll be poor, and Mantua is ugly and scary, but we could go anywhere."

"Ben, I can't run away with you. That isn't what I want."

"Tell me what you want, and I'll move the earth to get it for you."

"I want it all. I want to love you and love my family and my name that I'm proud of. And I want to take your name and love your family and be proud of that as well. I want a peaceful life of loving you, and I can't have that because of an ancient fight that I don't even know what it's about."

Benvolio held her tight as she wrapped her arms around him and buried her tearful face in his neck. He felt her heart beating fast. His love for her was strong. It was strong enough to sneak into the woods every night, strong enough to never care she was a Capulet. It had to be strong enough to stop her pain. He knew she was right. If he went to her parents now, it would be no different than what Romeo had done the night before. He understood that the only way to win Rosaline's hand in marriage was to end the fight, to find a way to stop the hate, to prove that love was enough. And with that hopeful thought, the cut on his arm singed with pain. Tybalt's rage was also strong, but Benvolio's love for Rosaline was stronger.

"This fight," he said, "has been fueled by hate for so many years. I'll put out this fire with love. Believe in me, my Rose. Look at me. I think you're right. The safest place for you right now is the nunnery. Go there and wait for me. I'll give you the peace and love you deserve."

She pulled him into a kiss. Her lips were warm, her skin soft on his. He felt her arms tighten around him, and her breath against his cheek was getting stronger. She was always so wild and free, but in his arms, she was calm. In her decision to join the nunnery, she was calm. And it was her resolve to have no man if she could not have him. That fueled Benvolio. He had to fight for her.

"I believe in you, Benvolio," she whispered in his ear, then kissed him. "They will be looking for me." She put his mask back over his eyes.

He made himself loosen his arms around her and let her go, for now. She rose up on her tiptoes and kissed him once more. Then she turned, put her mask on, and led him out from behind the tapestry. He followed her around the edge of the dance floor.

Benvolio could see only her. Her dark hair had fallen from her attempt to tie it up and was dancing on her shoulders as she walked. Her simple dress wrapped around her small waist and was falling softly on her hips as she moved gracefully through the crowd. She stopped and hid them behind a pillar. Tybalt was yelling at her uncle Lord Capulet in the middle of the party.

"It is him, Uncle. That villain Romeo is here," they heard Tybalt say.

"Calm down, nephew," Lord Capulet replied. "Don't you remember this morning? The prince told us to be civil. Besides, if that's Romeo, he is being a kind guest. If we need to find peace with the Montagues, I'm able to find it with that boy. Verona speaks very highly of him. They say he's a kind, pure, and polite young man and look at him. He means us no harm. Just enjoy the party. Look at me, Tybalt. Not for all the wealth in this town would I harm a Montague, more or less, and not a kind young man who happens to be a Montague in my home. Do you understand me? This is an order. Take note of him and be kind. Change your mood now and enjoy this party. The fight inside you is changing the atmosphere in here, so calm down now. Go and dance or something."

"The fight inside me is necessary when my enemy is a guest. I won't stand for this."

"You will stand down. Look at me. You will endure him. Am I the master here, or are you? If you fight that young man, you will ruin my party and upset my guests, creating another scene worse than the one you created this morning. And then it will be you who is my enemy."

"Uncle, how can you let this happen? It's a disgrace."

"Go and calm yourself down. You are being disobedient after all I've done for you. Ladies, come with me, let's dance.

Benvolio

Go, Tybalt, get some air and don't fight. Let me fill your glasses, ladies."

Benvolio quietly led Rosaline into the dance floor, staying out of Tybalt's sight.

"I'm guessing your parents haven't told your uncle about Romeo's confession of love for you last night."

"My parents will go to any length to keep their name clean, I suppose. My uncle will act civil to Romeo because he doesn't know about last night. And he will smile at you in the streets because he respects the prince."

"For whatever reason he smiles at me, I'll take it. I believe that the prince has finally gotten to him, and my uncle as well. Rosaline, did you hear him? He wants to have peace between us. I can take that smile he offers me in the streets and turn it into more."

"Oh, really? And what about Tybalt?"

"Is your uncle the master here, or is Tybalt?" He smiled at her. "Rosaline, my love for you is strong. It's pure and unbending. I'll love you every day of my life. I know this because I have loved you from the moment I chased you into the woods. I've never run so hard in my life as I did that day. And as you sat next to me on that root, you lifted your face, and it was wet with tears and dirt. What happened that afternoon, what keeps happening between our families, does not have to keep happening. I can stop it now. For whatever reason, your uncle is done fighting, and so is mine. I sat beside you on that root that day, and that was the moment for me, your smile and your mood-changing eyes. I fell in love with you that day, and I have loved you every day since, Rose."

"Oh, Benvolio, I love you," she said.

Her words sounded more like a good-bye than a confession of love. He held her as tightly as he could and moved slowly into the dance floor.

"Benvolio, look over there," she said.

She pointed behind him. On the edge of the dance floor, Benvolio could see Romeo with a girl.

"Is that Romeo?" she asked.

"It is," he said. "Do you know who the girl is? I can't tell with her mask on."

"That is Juliet."

"Your cousin Juliet?"

"Yes."

"Man, he really knows how to pick a girl."

"Come on. I want to hear what they're saying."

They snuck close to them and could hear them speak.

"Then stand still while my prayers come true," Romeo said.

He and Juliet disappeared behind a wall into a quiet dark hall. Benvolio and Rosaline followed without being seen.

Romeo whispered, "Now from my lips to yours, all my sins are purged."

Juliet responded, "Then it's my lips that are filled with your sins that now need to be purged."

"My sins?" Romeo said. "I can't let you carry my sins on your lips. I'll take them from you again with another kiss."

"They're kissing?" Benvolio asked.

"Yes!" Rosaline said.

"Well, it didn't take him long to get over you."

Rosaline elbowed him on the ribs.

"Do you know what this could mean?" Benvolio asked her. "If your uncle is willing to answer to the prince's command, and it's your uncle who has the power in the Capulet family, then perhaps it's not us who need to change your mother's heart. It's Romeo and Juliet who can open your uncle's eyes to see the power that love can have in ending this fight. Then, if they can get our uncles' blessing, they can't deny us their blessing as well."

"But it's Romeo. He was in love with me this morning, and now he is in love with Juliet."

"Maybe his heart needed a place to land. It wasn't welcomed by you, but it looks very welcomed by Juliet. Rose, do you see how this could work? Instead of me changing the mind of your mother, your uncle's open heart could allow his daughter to marry Romeo Montague; and if the master of your family allows it, your mother will have to follow suit."

"I love to see you filled with hope. Maybe you're right about Romeo's heart. He's so full of love, and it looks like Juliet feels the same way. Benvolio, I have to go now."

"Rosaline, please don't let this be good-bye. Not now that I finally have you in my arms. Not now that I finally found the courage to tell you I love you. I was a fool not to confess my love for you the moment I first saw you. Let me tell you, let me show you every day from here on out that I love you."

"I see my mother looking for me. She's ready to leave. Benvolio, I believe you can move the earth for me. Keep your sword in your sheath, and I believe if anyone can find peace between the Capulets and the Montagues, it will be you. When you do, you will know where to find me, not married to my father's choice of a man but simply finding peace in this world the only way I know how. Push Romeo down this path. Give him the strength to love Juliet. And know that I will always love you."

She stole one last kiss from him and disappeared into the crowd.

"I'll fight for you, my Rose," he yelled. After seeing the attention his holler received, he slipped away and landed directly at Mercutio's table.

"Ben, welcome," Mercutio said. "Tell me, did you find her? Did you get to have her one last time before she marries Jesus?"

"You're drunk, Mercutio," Benvolio said as he took a seat and stole Mercutio's drink for himself.

"And you're not. Let's fix that." He ordered another round.

"Thank you, Mercutio, for tonight and for not saying anything to Romeo today about Rosaline."

They received two drinks and tossed them back in a single swallow.

"It killed me not to say anything," Mercutio said. "I told you this would happen. He was never going to catch you in the middle of the night at the edge of the woods with her. I'm the only one clever enough to do that. And I told you, if he never knows that you love her, he would fall madly in love with her himself. Oh God, it took everything I had not to say something."

"Right. Well, thanks."

"Thank me again tomorrow. I won't remember this moment. Where is that Romeo anyway? Did he find relief for his pain?"

"I think he might have."

Two more drinks landed on their table, and they threw them back as well. Benvolio sat silently, watching the hall where he'd left Romeo and Juliet. A few more drinks arrived and disappeared quickly. He looked to the dance floor and noticed that the crowd had thinned out.

"Madam, your mother would like to speak with you," he heard a nurse holler as she approached Romeo and Juliet's hiding place.

"It's time for us to go, Mercutio," Benvolio said. He quickly got up and moved toward Romeo.

"Who is her mother?" he heard Romeo ask the nurse.

Emily Whitaker

The nurse answered, "Why, young man, her mother is the lady of the house. She is a wise and amazing woman. However, it was I who nursed the young lady you were talking to. Let that be known, and let me tell you another thing, young man. Whoever is lucky enough to marry that amazing young lady will be walking away with a hefty sum of money."

"She is a Capulet then? My costly heart, am I destined to always love what I can never have?"

The nurse left him with an awkward smile.

Benvolio put his arm around Romeo quickly and said, "Come on, Romeo, let's go. This party is over."

"I'm afraid it is, Benvolio, along with so much more."

Benvolio knew this was the moment he needed to start pushing Romeo toward Juliet. But Benvolio's head was spinning. He rubbed his face and brushed his hands through his hair. He readjusted his mask and stepped outside. Taking in the fresh air, he tried to collect his thoughts.

"Listen to me," he said, turning back toward Romeo. "Romeo? Where did he go?"

6

Most of the party's guests were crowded outside, waiting for their carriages to come. The moon had shifted in the sky, and its light was blocked by the Capulet villa. Benvolio looked out into the vast green lawns from the steps and saw nothing but darkness.

"Where is Romeo?" he said, swirling around a little too quickly.

Once the crowd stopped spinning around him, he focused his eyes. Beside him stood Mercutio, who was silently staring forward, teetering from side to side and holding his hand in front of him as if there were still a cup of wine in it.

"Mercutio, have you seen Romeo?" Benvolio asked.

"Yes," he said, falling forward a bit with his nod.

"You have? Where?"

"He's with Benvolio."

"Oh, come on, you fool. We have to find him."

"Benvolio?" Mercutio yelled. "Oh, I found him. Here you are. Let's go," Mercutio said, heading for the gates.

"No, this way," Benvolio said, dragging Mercutio into the dark lawns of the villa.

"What are we doing?"

"Looking for Romeo."

"In the dark?"

"Romeo," Benvolio hollered. "My cousin, Romeo. ROMEO!"

"He is a smart man, Benvolio. I bet you he's left us to go home and crawl into bed."

"No, I bet he ran this way and then, and then, listen. I bet he jumped over this orchard wall here. Call him. Do it. Call him, Mercutio."

"Why would I call him Mercutio? No, I'll make him come to us by using other names. Romeo! Humours! Madman! Passion! Lover!" Mercutio hollered as he stumbled on the grass. "Come stand before me as you do with your heavy sighs of love. Speak a poem to me, and I'll know it's you. Say words like *Ay me* and *love* and *dove* and—wow, I tripped on that. Don't trip on that. There, do you see it?" His nose almost touched the grass to see the tiny pebble he had tripped over.

"Romeo," Mercutio hopped up and screamed. "Come speak to my good friend here, the goddess of love and beauty. Only one word, and she will take that word to her confident son, Cupid, with his perfect aim, like in that song 'King Cophetua.' Do you remember that song? It's a good song, Romeo, where a king loves a maid who lives on the streets."

Mercutio teetered on his feet, waiting for an answer. "Benvolio, he isn't here. He can't hear me. He won't come to us. Oh, I've got it. He is playing dead, and I need to breathe life back into him. That's probably it. Let me see. Just let me see. Oh, Romeo, I have Rosaline here with me! I'll prove it. I'm looking at her beautiful blue eyes, her queenlike big forehead, and her deep-red lips."

"Hey, that's enough, Mercutio," Benvolio said as he fell toward Mercutio, trying to make him stop.

Mercutio leapt away from him again and again. "Oh, right. I mean her beautiful feet, her long smooth legs, and as you move up those legs, her thighs quiver."

"Mercutio," Benvolio yelled, trying to chase after him.

"Sorry, sorry." Mercutio stopped and tried to catch his breath. "And I guess, Romeo, whatever else you loved about the fair Rosaline is right here. So just come out and head home with us."

"You really think talking about his old love will make him want to come with us? If anything, wow." Benvolio stumbled. "If anything, you just made him mad."

"What do you mean, I've made him mad? He gets angry at the beauty that is his love? And at the idea of loving a woman until he is satisfied? That's a stupid thing to be mad about, Benvolio. I'm right, I know it. The name of his love will make him come to us."

"Come on, Mercutio. I bet he's hiding himself in these trees by this wall. I bet he found comfort in the dark because it matches his mood. His love will never see happiness as he still hopes it will, so why not hide in the dark woods?" Benvolio said. He stopped and sat down where there was no bench and fell. He knew he was moving closer to Rosaline's window and found it comforting to sit in the shadows and sulk.

Mercutio waddled over and plopped down beside him. "If Cupid were blind, his arrows would never hit his mark," he said. "And neither will Romeo sit under a medlar tree and wish his love was that kind of fruit instead of the kind she is."

"What?"

"Maids call medlar fruit open-arse. Hah, Romeo, I wish for you that she was an open-arse and you were a poperin pear."

"Are you talking about fruit?"

"You're right, Benvolio, I'm done. Romeo! Wherever you are, good night. I'm going to my bed, only because this field is too cold for me to sleep in. Come on, Benvolio, let's go."

"Yes, we should go. We'll never find him when he doesn't want to be found."

"This way then." Mercutio pointed toward where they came but did not get up from his spot beside Benvolio.

Slowly he started to sink until his head was resting on the cool ground.

"Mercutio, no," Benvolio said, making his way to his feet. "Get up. Come on, we're still on Capulet land."

He pulled on Mercutio and tried to shake him awake, but he failed and fell back to the ground. Trying to focus his fuzzy mind, he sat in silence until he heard a noise in the distance. He held his breath so he could hear it clearly. He stood and quietly ventured toward the voice.

"They laugh at me when they've never even felt the pain of love," it said.

Benvolio recognized the voice. It was Romeo's. He was in the Capulet gardens after all.

"Wait," Romeo said, making Benvolio stop in place. "What is that new light coming from that window?"

Romeo hadn't seen Benvolio; he was talking to himself. Benvolio let Romeo speak. He wanted to hear if he would talk of Juliet or of Rosaline.

"Oh, if that light were the east, then Juliet would be the sun," Romeo said.

He was speaking of Juliet. Benvolio wanted to give him this time to solidify his love for Juliet. Stepping back, Benvolio took a seat on the boulder behind him. From there, he was able to keep an eye on Romeo in case a Capulet guard came along.

"Rise, beautiful sun," Romeo continued. "And kill the envious moon with your light. The goddess of the moon and

Emily Whitaker

of virginity is Diana. She is pale and ill with grief because you are more beautiful than her. Do not be her maid, Juliet. She is jealous. Her virginity makes her sick and green. It is only a fool that holds on to virginity. Juliet, let it go."

"What are you saying?" Benvolio whispered, laughing to himself. He was thankful Mercutio was not awake for this.

Romeo ran and climbed the towering wall that Mercutio was asleep against. Benvolio was stunned. It was the wall to Juliet's private garden and chambers. He couldn't believe what Romeo was trying to do.

"Romeo," he whispered loudly. He was suddenly aware of the danger they were in.

Romeo didn't answer, so he climbed the wall after him. He struggled up the wall, still clumsy with drink. He swung his leg over the top, and once he was stable, he looked for Romeo, who was in the garden looking up at the balcony. Benvolio followed his gaze and saw Juliet. He hugged the wall so he wouldn't fall off in terror. He wanted to call for Romeo to run, but he figured he couldn't call him without Juliet noticing.

"Oh, it's Juliet in the window," Romeo said softly. "My Juliet, it is my love."

"Romeo, be quiet," Benvolio whispered.

"Oh, I wish she knew that she was my love."

"Romeo, can you hear me? Get out of there."

But Romeo could not hear him.

"Wait," Romeo continued. "She's speaking. No, it was only a sigh. What is she thinking about? Her eyes look like she's thinking of love. I'll speak to her of love."

"Romeo," Benvolio whispered.

But he wanted Romeo to talk to her. He wanted him to approach her and confess his love for her. He knew Romeo would never get another chance.

"Wait, what am I doing?" Romeo said. "I'm too bold to think it's me that she loves. Oh, but her eyes shine so brightly, like two stars from above that have taken their place on her face. And yet the brightness of her cheeks shames the stars of her eyes, as the light of the sun does to the light of a lamp. And still her eyes shine through that light with such brightness that if she were an angel, they would shine through the clouds, and the birds would sing to them as if they were the sun. Look at how she sets her cheek upon her hand. Oh, I wish I were a glove on her hand so I could be resting against her cheek."

"Ay me." Juliet sighed.

Benvolio sat up and scooted back into the shadow of a tree. He knew this could go one of two ways. Either he would need to help Romeo escape, or she would be happy to see him. Benvolio was ready for both.

"She speaks," Romeo whispered. "Oh, keep speaking, bright angel. You are the most beautiful creature of the night. You are like an angel flying to the earth as people watch you with wide eyes. The people fall back as they gaze up at the angel who flies through the air."

Benvolio held in a bit of laughter.

"Oh, Romeo, Romeo," Juliet said. "Where have you gone to, my Romeo? Forget your name of Montague. Deny it, deny your family and father. Or if you won't, I'll swear my love for you and deny my name. I'll no longer be a Capulet."

Benvolio was stunned.

"Should I keep listening?" Romeo asked. "Or should I speak to her?"

"It's only your name that is my enemy," she continued. "Romeo is not my enemy. He would still be my Romeo if he had any other name. What power does the name Montague hold anyway? It isn't something you can touch or see. It's not a hand or a foot or arm or face or any other part belonging to a man's body. Oh, I wish he had any other name. Why is a name so important anyway? If you call a rose by any other name, it will still smell as sweet. It is still red, and it is still as beautiful, just as Romeo would be with any other name. So be the beautiful Romeo with a different name than Montague and take me to replace the name that you've left behind."

Benvolio worried what Romeo was thinking in the shadows, hearing his new love talk of the hate between their families and asking him to leave his family to love her. He wanted to jump down and explain that it didn't have to be that way. But before he could do anything, Romeo spoke loudly.

"I will, Juliet," Romeo said, coming out of the shadows. "Declare your love for only me, and I'll newly baptize myself with any other name for you. From this moment forward, I'll no longer be Romeo."

"Who is that down there?" Juliet gasped. "Have you been listening to me speak?"

Benvolio was ready to help Romeo run.

"I can't tell you who I am because my name is the name of your enemy, and for that reason, I hate my name. If I had it written on a piece of paper, I would tear it up to prove it to you."

"I have not had the chance to hear your voice speak more than one hundred words, and still I recognize the sound of it. You are Romeo, and you are a Montague," Juliet answered.

"I'll be none of those if they bring you any pain, my beautiful Juliet."

"Romeo, how did you get to my balcony? The walls are so high, and if my kinsmen found you here, the punishment would be death because you are a Montague."

"I flew over your high walls with Cupid's wings of love. Not even walls made of stone could keep me away from you," he said as he leapt toward her balcony and began to climb. "And for that same reason, you don't need to worry about your kinsmen. They can't catch my flying heart."

Benvolio chuckled. Romeo was so smooth.

"You don't understand, Romeo," Juliet said. "If they even see you, they will kill you."

He had climbed to the edge of her balcony and was inches away from her face. "Your eyes are filling with worry," he said. "Look at me with love again, and I'll be armored against the swords of your kinsmen."

"I can't. I'm too scared that they'll see you here."

"My Juliet, I have the darkness of night to hide in. Besides, if you don't love me, then let them find me. Because I would rather die than live in a world without your love."

She stood still for a moment then let herself fall into his arms. She held him to the side of her balcony as he kissed her softly.

"Romeo," she said, her head resting against his. "How did you find me?"

"I was led here by love," he said. "He told me where to go, and with his guidance, I found you. I would have found you if you were on the shore of the sea on the other end of the earth. And I would travel as far to be by your side."

"It's dark tonight, Romeo. If there were light, you would see that I'm blushing. I realize you've heard everything I've said to myself tonight." She pulled away from him. "Oh, I should happily follow the formal way to express my feelings for you. Oh, forget it." She rushed back to his arms, and they kissed and held each other tightly. "Romeo, do you love me? I know you will say yes, and I'll believe you. But

Benvolio

just because you say it doesn't make it true. Oh, Romeo, if you do love me, say it and mean it."

Juliet pulled away playfully. "Or if you think I'm too easy and you want a chase, I'll turn away from you and say no so you can work hard to convince me to love you. But I don't want to do that. The truth is, my beautiful enemy, Romeo Montague, I love you. And I'm sure that because I have said all this, you think I'm silly, a girl who falls for any man who gives her attention. But trust me, Romeo. I'll prove to you that I love you truly, and I won't waste my time with games. Perhaps I should—I know that's how it's done. But you've already heard me speak of my love for you, so I won't waste our time with what is proper. You know I love you, Romeo."

Benvolio almost lost his grip on the wall. Juliet loved Romeo, and Romeo was obviously in love with her.

Romeo pulled her back to him. "Juliet, believe in my love for you," he said. "Do you see how the moon shines bright and paints the tips of the trees with silver?"

"Oh, don't swear your love to me by the moon," Juliet said. "The moon changes constantly every month. Unless that's what you're saying of your love for me, that it will change constantly."

"No, I'm not, but then what should I swear by?"

"Don't swear by anything, or if you must, swear on yourself. Because you are everything to me, and I believe in you, Romeo."

"Then, my heart's dear love—"

"Wait, don't swear at all. Although I'm full of joy that you love me, I don't enjoy making a contract tonight like this. It's too rash. It's not a good idea. We're moving too fast, fast like lightning, which before you can say 'Look at that bolt of lightning,' it's gone forever. So I'm going to say good night, sweet Romeo. This brand-new love can grow as spring eases into summer, and as it does, it can prove itself to be a strong, beautiful love, as a spring bud blooms into a summer flower. For now, good night. Let your heart rest knowing how I love you."

He pulled her in and kissed her. The soft touch of his kiss slowly filled with passion. Juliet stopped him and smiled. She kissed his cheek and turned to go inside.

"You can't leave me so unsatisfied," Romeo called after her.

"Excuse me, Romeo," she said. "But what satisfaction did you expect from me tonight?"

Benvolio held his breath.

"I only want to leave knowing that you love me as much as I love you," Romeo said.

"I've already told you I love you before you asked me to," Juliet said. "Though I wish I could take it back and say it for the first time again."

"Would you take back what you've said about our love? Why?"

"I would only take it back to give you even more of my love in greater quantities," Juliet said. "But here I am, wishing for what I already have. My gift in giving you my love is as endless as the sea. And my love for you is as deep. The more I give to you, the more I'm given in return, making our love endless. I hear someone inside, dear love. I have to go. I'm coming, Nurse," she yelled inside, then turned back to Romeo. "Stay where you are, Romeo, and wait for me. I'll come back in a moment."

As Juliet disappeared into her room, Romeo held on to the side of the balcony and attempted to hide behind a vine. "Oh, blessed night," he said. "Because of your darkness, I'm scared that all of this is a dream. It's too good to be true."

Benvolio wanted to call out to him, but Juliet had returned.

"Three words, dear Romeo," she said. "And then we must say good-night. If your love for me is true, and you mean to marry me, send word to me tomorrow by a messenger that I'll choose and send your way. Tell my messenger where and what time our marriage ceremony will take place, and everything that's mine will be yours. I'll follow you throughout the world."

"Madam," said the nurse from inside.

"I'm coming, Nurse. But, Romeo, if you don't intend to marry me, I'm begging you—"

"Madam," the nurse called.

"I'm coming right now. Hold on." She turned back to Romeo. "Please stop all of this and don't seek me out again and leave me to my grief. Tomorrow I'll send for you."

"I'm determined with all of my soul," Romeo said, wrapping his arms around her and holding her for another kiss.

"I wish I could stand here and tell you good-night a thousand times," she said.

She turned, and though it was so obvious that she wanted to stay, she pushed herself inside. Romeo made his way off the balcony wall.

"I wish it were day," Romeo said to himself. "And I could vow my love to you. I'm meant to be near you. I'm drawn to you with love."

Benvolio saw the curtains open, and Juliet came out again.

"Oh, how I wish I had a falconer's voice to call my male falcon back again. But like the falcon, I'm not free, and so I must whisper. Because if I could call out your name, I would say it over and over again until I had torn a hole in Echo's cave, where she dwells and makes her voice even more hoarse than mine, repeating, 'My Romeo!'"

Romeo heard her and ran back to the balcony, climbing the wall with ease.

"Oh, it's my soul you call to when you say my name," he said, startling her a bit. "How sweet your words are in this night, like soft music to my ears."

"Romeo."

"My love."

She held his face and kissed him. "What time tomorrow shall I send my messenger to you?" she asked him.

"By the hour of nine in the morning."

"I won't fail you. It is forever until then. I've forgotten why I have called you back."

"Let me stay here until you remember it."

"I'll never remember with you here. All I can think of is how I love your company."

"And I'll still stay, even if you never remember. Because I've forgotten any other home but this."

"It's almost morning. I know you need to go, but I don't want you to."

"I wish I never had to leave your side," he said.

"So do I, and yet I would kill you if I were to make you stay. Good night, good night. I hate to see you go, so I'll only say good night and hope to see you as my husband tomorrow."

"Sleep rests upon your eyes as peace is in your breast. I wish I were sleep and peace. But now, I'll rush off to my friar's cell. I'll tell him of my love, and I'll ask him for his help."

Romeo reluctantly came down from the balcony and turned to climb the wall that Benvolio was sitting on. Stunned at what he just heard, Benvolio couldn't move. Had his cousin just promised to marry Juliet Capulet? Benvolio looked down and saw Romeo leap onto the wall and climb up it. Speechless, Benvolio sat there in the shadows as Romeo passed inches away without seeing him and climbed down the other side.

Romeo was halfway across the Capulet gardens before Benvolio regained use of himself. He silently crawled down the wall and found his way back to Mercutio.

"Mercutio, get up," he whispered. Mercutio didn't budge. "Come on, the sun is coming up. We can't be found in the Capulet gardens."

Benvolio pulled and pushed him, but he didn't move. As Benvolio stood, he saw the sun's light was filling the gardens. He desperately kicked Mercutio, who didn't respond. Benvolio turned to the outer wall and saw the tree branch that reached across the high wall to its mate.

"Mercutio? Come on," he said, pulling him once more. "Fine. Oh, you are going to kill me when I see you next."

Benvolio left him in the grass and ran toward the tree. He leapt to its lowest branch and began to climb. But before he swung onto the branch reaching over the wall, he turned to see Rosaline's window. Her life would change when she awoke, and she had no idea how much.

"You will join the nunnery tomorrow, my love, but I'll find you, and I'll tell you to keep hope in your heart. Love between our families is more possible than you can imagine."

He turned and jumped out of the Capulet gardens.

7

Running around the outer edge of the Capulet wall and through the woods, Benvolio came around the corner. He looked for Romeo but couldn't see him. He ran to the Capulet gates and peered inside. Romeo was still making his way out of the gardens.

"Hurry up. Get out of there before you get caught," Benvolio said under his breath.

Romeo was prancing on without a care in the world and finally came to a tree. He swung up onto the wall to climb out of the gardens. Benvolio turned to walk into town as if it were a coincidence he was there. But then he remembered Romeo's plans to visit Friar Lawrence. Benvolio had to make sure the friar would help with Romeo and Juliet's wedding. He ran, and when he got to the church, he went around the back to Friar Lawrence's cell.

"Friar Lawrence?" Benvolio called, gasping for breath.

Emily Whitaker

The friar's cell was simple. His bed sat on the floor, and a table with a bowl of water stood in the corner. A cross was the only break in the bleak gray walls of stone and mud. He was praying beside his bed. His earth-colored cloak was tight around his large belly, and his gray hair was thinning at the cap of his head. He looked up at Benvolio, who was standing in his doorway.

"Benvolio, my son, you're up early to pray," the friar said, laughing to himself. He stood. "I'm mistaken. You're up late, very late."

"I am, Friar, and I'll pray. But please, I don't have long to speak with you."

"What is it, my boy?"

"It's about the fight between my family and the Capulets."

"Oh yes, it's weighing heavily on this town. I know it has always burdened you, Benvolio."

"Do you remember how you told me that fighting hate would never bring peace?"

"I do. We agreed that it will only fuel the fire further."

"Do you remember when I asked you if love could be strong enough to end the fight?"

"I do, my son, and when you asked me, I had hope that you would do something with such a great idea."

"Right." Benvolio looked at the ground. "It's just that I...well, just listen to me. Romeo is on his way to you now. Please remember the power that love could have when he asks for what he needs from you."

Benvolio

"Benvolio, I don't understand. What does young Romeo need from me?"

"Promise me, Friar?"

"I promise you, my son. I promise."

"And don't tell him I was here. He doesn't know that I know, and I think it's best I let him tell me on his own."

"Tell you what?"

"Promise me you will go along with what he needs."

"If it has anything to do with peace and love between your families, you have my word that I will help in whatever way I can. But I don't understand, what will Romeo ask me for?"

"Thank you, Friar, thank you."

Benvolio ran out of the friar's cell. The sunlight blinded him. He tried to see if Romeo was near, but no one was walking about. His head was blurry, so he turned to go home.

With his muddy shoes and clothes from the night before, he decided it was best to sneak through the servants' door in the kitchen. No one was there, so he ran up the stairs and into his room. Looking at his bed, he wished he could jump into it and sleep away the day, but today was too important. He had to change and get back to town. He needed to be where Romeo could find him and tell him about his new love. He also had to see Rosaline before she entered the church. He had to tell her what had happened with Romeo and Juliet.

He changed his clothes and got the mud off his boots. He washed his face with the water in the bowl and tried to tame his hair. He heard a clatter from the kitchen, and his stomach began to rumble. He ran back down the stairs and into the kitchen. Heat was coming from the brick ovens, and the smell of eggs and butter wafted through the air. Benvolio grabbed an apple to tide him over until the real food was ready. He joined Balthazar, who was washing out a greasy barrel.

"Good, Balthazar, you're awake," Benvolio said.

"Of course, I'm awake," Balthazar said. "How was the party? Did Romeo find a beauty that could end his love for that Capulet nun?"

"I, well, I don't know. I lost track of him last night." He leaned against the wall and watched Balthazar work.

"What do you mean you lost track of him?" Balthazar said. "Neither one of you came home last night."

"Oh, Romeo didn't come home?" Benvolio awkwardly looked at his apple instead of Balthazar.

"I swear, if he spent last night walking through the woods pining over that Jesus-loving Capulet, I swear—"

"Wow, those are some strong words. All right! Calm down."

"A letter arrived for Romeo this morning."

Benvolio stood and tossed his apple away. "Let me see it," he said, wiping his hands on his chest.

"Why?" Balthazar said, pulling the letter out of his pocket.

"Look, it has the seal of Capulet on it. Open it. What does it say?"

Balthazar opened the letter, held it up, and squinted.

"Right, sorry," Benvolio said. "Give it to me."

"What does it say?" Balthazar asked.

"It is a challenge for Romeo to fight Tybalt."

"Tybalt wants to fight Romeo? That arrogant bastard wants to fight Romeo because he knows he will win. He needs to save his pride after you humiliated him yesterday."

"I did not humiliate him. I wasn't even fighting him, Balthazar. I was trying to keep the peace."

"Right, by putting Tybalt in his rightful place!"

"That is not—listen to me, Balthazar. Tybalt wants to fight Romeo because last night at the party, he recognized him."

"Tybalt knew Romeo was in his home at his party, and now Romeo is missing?"

"No, he isn't missing. Listen, Tybalt told his uncle that Romeo was at the party and that he wanted to take care of it, but Lord Capulet told him to let it go. He said that if Tybalt acted against Romeo and ruined his party, he would be severely punished. Tybalt must have listened since he didn't go after Romeo last night. I know that."

"How do you know that?"

"Because I just do, because of this note, challenging Romeo to a duel today in the town square. Do you send a proper invitation when you've already finished the job the night before?"

"You do if you're trying to cover your tracks. Fine. Look, if you're right, then we don't have to worry. Romeo won't 'dance' with Tybalt. He will keep the peace in his answer to him. He's no fighter, so just leave it alone, Ben."

"Normally you know I would. But in this case, there's too much to lose. Come with me. We have to find Romeo and help him keep the peace." Then Benvolio called for the head serving woman. "Ma'am?"

"Yes, sir," she answered.

"I need Balthazar to help me fetch some goods from the market. I'll have him back shortly."

Benvolio and Balthazar ran out the door before she could object.

"What do you mean there is too much to lose?" Balthazar asked as they ran toward town.

"I mean that, well, the prince has put a penalty of death on any who fight in the name of Capulet or Montague."

"But Romeo wouldn't fight, so it would end in Tybalt's death. I like it. What's the problem?"

"The problem is Tybalt could kill Romeo as he stands refusing to fight, and then he would be sent to death."

"Oh, man, you're right."

They sped up.

8

As the two ran into town, Benvolio heard a familiar voice.

"Benvolio," Mercutio called out. He was leaning against the wall of a tavern in a bit of shade. "A word, if you please."

"Oh, Mercutio. Listen, I—"

"Benvolio, please explain to me why I woke this morning in the dew-covered grass of the Capulet gardens?"

"You woke up in the Capulet gardens?" Balthazar said, trying not to laugh.

"Yes, boy, I did, next to a pool of my own sick, against the wall of their only daughter's chambers. If I were caught, I would have been killed."

"I tried to move you," Benvolio said. "I tried to wake you, but you were out cold. I had to leave you there. Besides, they would never kill a family member of the prince."

"Their only daughter's chambers, Benvolio! How could I possibly explain that to the prince?"

"What were you guys doing in the Capulet gardens?" Balthazar asked.

"Tempting fate," Mercutio said. "No, wait, what were we doing in their gardens? Were we hunting down Romeo?"

"We were being drunken fools, and that's all. We wanted to find Romeo, but there was no reason to believe he would be in their gardens."

"No, we did find Romeo back there. I remember hearing his dreamy voice spouting about love and heartsick poetry and feelings."

"We did not find anything. You remember a drunken dream."

"Are you telling me that I dreamt about Romeo spouting love poems to me as I slept in my own sick?"

"Yes, I am."

"Okay, then. But Romeo was missing," Mercutio said.

"He is missing, and now we need to find him," Balthazar said.

"He is not missing, but we do need to find him," Benvolio said. "Tybalt saw him at the party last night and has challenged him to a duel."

"Romeo in a duel with Tybalt? The punishment is death either way," Mercutio said.

"That's why we need to find Romeo. We need to make sure he doesn't fight Tybalt."

"Did Romeo come home at all last night?" Mercutio asked.

"No," Balthazar said.

"No? Well, it was probably that coldhearted wench Rosaline that still has a hold on his heart. She torments him so much that I'm sure he'll go mad."

"It's not Rosaline," Benvolio yelled. "I mean, it's Tybalt we need to worry about now."

"Tybalt wants a challenge. Then I'll answer him," Mercutio said.

"Romeo will answer Tybalt calmly with us behind him. Mercutio, listen to me. There cannot be any more fighting. I'm serious."

"Oh please, Benvolio, you're always trying to keep the peace. But any man who can write a letter can answer Tybalt."

"No, Mercutio. Romeo will answer Tybalt's letter, and I know Romeo will not fight him. He will find a way to keep the peace, and we will do whatever we can to help him."

"Oh, poor Romeo, he's already dead. He's fallen in love with a woman he can't have, and for that, he will suffer a fate worse than death. He is a heartbroken lover, and in no way is he man enough to answer Tybalt's challenge."

"Right, well, that's exactly why he needs our help. Come on, both of you," Benvolio said as he led them toward the church. They stopped to search the crowd. "Keep an eye out for Tybalt and Romeo."

"Why are we looking for them here?" Balthazar asked.

"It's the bottleneck of the town. One of them has to come through here to find the other."

Benvolio hoped that Romeo was still inside the church, making plans for his marriage to Juliet with the friar. He wanted Romeo to come out and see them. He wanted him to run to them and finally tell him about Juliet so he could stop being so secretive. He stood with Mercutio and Balthazar, arms crossed and eyes focused. Benvolio noticed the people of the town glaring back at them with looks of warning and concern.

"Relax, guys, we don't want the people of Verona to think we are looking for a fight here," Benvolio said.

Mercutio took a seat on the stone base of a statue. Balthazar leaned against it, and Benvolio could only manage to uncross his arms. He took a deep breath and continued to search the crowd. He looked toward the Capulet villa to see if Tybalt was headed their way. The gates were open in the distance, but it was Lady Capulet coming through them. Her dark dress was large but had no sparkle to it, a blatant display, as if to state she were in mourning. She stopped suddenly and turned. Rosaline was coming up behind her in the same plain dress as the night before, with her hair softly pulled back. Her mother grabbed her violently by the arm. Instinctively Benvolio started to run toward her. He could see no crowd, no church, no sky—only her face, wet with tears. And then her eyes met his. She smiled at him for a moment and then called out.

"Stop," she said calmly.

Benvolio

Benvolio stopped. Rosaline took her arm out of her mother's grasp and stood tall. She smiled at him and then at her mother. She pointed herself toward the church, and with her shoulders back, she began to walk.

"Come, Mother. We have made promises, and we need to stick to them now," she said loudly, shooting one last smile at Benvolio.

Her mother scurried after her. Benvolio walked back to stand with Mercutio and Balthazar.

"What the hell was that?" Mercutio asked, not truly paying attention.

"I thought I saw Tybalt," Benvolio answered.

"Oh yes, and charging at him is the best way to not fight him. I like this plan. I think it's solid."

"Look, I'm worried Tybalt will find Romeo before we do. What if they are fighting somewhere right now? Should we search for him? We could split up."

"Enough. Sit down and relax."

They sat in silence. Benvolio started to think of his cousin in an alley, facing Tybalt by himself. He was sure Romeo would lose to Tybalt, based only on the fact that he loved too much. Tybalt's hate would overpower him. But Romeo knew how to fight, so why was he so sure Romeo would lose?

"Romeo is an accomplished fighter, right? Why do you think he would lose a fight against Tybalt?" Benvolio asked Mercutio.

The question sent Mercutio leaping through the crowd. He put on a show as he spoke of the talent Tybalt had with his sword. Benvolio was entertained but never stopped looking for Romeo. It wasn't long into Mercutio's display that Romeo finally emerged from the church.

"Enough, Mercutio. Here comes Romeo," Benvolio called out.

"Yes, but without his Rose," Mercutio said, still putting on a show, thrusting himself toward Romeo.

"This isn't about Rosaline anymore, Mercutio. Shut your mouth."

"No, but apparently everything is about her with you," Mercutio said, then turned to Romeo. "Did our lover get to love last night? And in the act become an empty fish? He is left with only a ME! And an 'O, Ro-me-o!' Now he lives in the verses of Petrarch, an Italian poet who wrote of a woman named Laura. Compare her to Romeo's Rosaline, and she was a kitchen wench with a better chance of love. For love is tragic. Look at Cleopatra, Helen, Hero, Thisbe— so tragic. And then there is Romeo. Signor Romeo, bonjour. There is a French greeting to replace the French words that I truly wish I could speak to you. You ditched us last night."

Benvolio began to calm down. They were with Romeo in front of the church, surrounded by townspeople. When Tybalt found them, they would be able to work everything out peacefully.

"I'm sorry, Mercutio," Romeo said. "My reason for leaving you was very important. And in a case like this, a man is allowed to abandon his friends."

"So you mean to say that a case like yours allows a man to stop being polite? He bows out from his friends to bow into his business?" Mercutio said.

Romeo smiled, and Benvolio could see that his cousin had finally returned to the playful boy who could float on love instead of drown beneath it.

"You mean I should curtsy?" Romeo said.

"That is exactly what I mean, Romeo," said Mercutio.

"What a courteous way to begin the day."

"Yes, well, I'm very courteous. In fact, I'm so courteous that I'm the very pink of courtesy."

"Pink of courtesy? Like a flower?"

"Yes, Romeo, pink like a flower on a well-decorated shoe."

"Well, that would explain my well-decorated pump."

"Oh, you want to be the witty one now?" Mercutio said, circling him playfully. "Well, see if you can keep up with me on this joke until your pump is all worn-out. And then, when the sole is worn down, nothing but the joke will remain. Leave one single sole left."

"But, Mercutio, this isn't a good joke. It's only unique because it's such a weak joke. In the end, it will be the only joke left because it's the worst of its kind."

"Come between us, good Benvolio. My wits are fading with this man."

Emily Whitaker

"Oh, come on, Mercutio," Romeo said. "You can do better than this. Challenge me, or I'll declare myself the winner of this match."

Benvolio enjoyed having his happy cousin back. It was clear that everything had gone well with the friar. Though the next move was Juliet's, Romeo didn't seem worried, so Benvolio decided not to worry either.

Mercutio began to dance around Romeo. "No," he said. "If our wits are to run this wild-goose chase, on this wild course you've chosen, then I'm done. You have more wild geese in one of your wits than I have in five. Have I won this match yet by babbling on about a goose?"

"Oh, Mercutio, I have never known you not to be the goose," Romeo countered. "I can always count on you to play the fool."

"Then as a goose, I'll bite your ear."

"Please, good goose, don't."

Mercutio chased Romeo through the crowd.

"Your wit is very playful and sweet, Romeo," Mercutio said.

"Then shall I use it to sweeten your goose?"

"You are stretching this one a little broad."

"It is the word *broad* that I'll stretch it for. And when you add the word *broad* to the word *goose*, are you not a broad goose?" Romeo laughed at his own joke.

"Oh yeah, good one, Romeo. Come on, isn't this better than when he was groaning on about a woman? Now you're actually fun. You're Romeo again. That love you held on to made you an idiot, running around trying to hide your sword in a hole."

"All right," Benvolio said. "Stop there."

"Benvolio, you are asking me to stop just as I'm getting started on my tale of the hare?" Mercutio said.

"If I let you keep going, your tale will grow too large. Enough, Mercutio."

"No, you are wrong. I would have made it short because I have already made my point. And I have come to the end of my tale," he said, using his sword to make his point.

"Oh, lighten up, you two," Romeo said. "Wow, here we go. Look at that. It's a sail, a sail."

Coming at them from the Capulet villa was a large blue sail of sorts. The hat stood taller than the woman beneath it, causing her form to take the shape of a single large moving object. Beside her stood a small man running to keep up. As the duo approached the boys, Benvolio could see it was Juliet's nurse.

Mercutio turned to her and started in. "The two of them," he said. "A shirt and a smock prancing along as if they didn't look absolutely ridiculous."

"Peter," the nurse said. Her voice was shrill, a drastic contradiction to her plump figure and kind face.

"Yeah, what?" Peter said.

Emily Whitaker

Benvolio immediately recognized Peter as the serving boy they had helped to read the guest list for the masquerade. Peter, however, had no recollection of Benvolio or Romeo.

"My fan, Peter," the nurse said.

"Oh yes, please, Peter," Mercutio said. "Give the woman her fan to hide her face. For the fan is the prettier of the two."

"Good morning, gentlemen," the nurse said.

"Good afternoon, fair gentlewoman," Mercutio answered.

"Is it afternoon already?"

"It is, I tell you, for the long hand of the dial is on the prick of noon." Mercutio teased the nurse's large dress with his sword.

"Get away from me. It's nine in the morning. What kind of man are you?"

"I am made in God's image, kind gentlewoman."

"Sure, 'in God's image,' he says. Gentlemen, do any of you know where I can find the young Romeo?"

"I can tell you," Romeo said. "But he will no longer be as young when I tell you as when you asked." Romeo laughed again at his own wit. "I'm the youngest of the name Romeo."

"Are you now?" the nurse asked.

Benvolio realized he was holding his breath. He wanted to step in and make sure they treated Juliet's nurse with respect, but he looked at her face and saw a smile. If there was one thing he could always trust his cousin with, it was sweet-talking any kind of woman. So he stood back and let Romeo be Romeo.

"Yes," Mercutio said, stepping in. "He is your young Romeo. However, I don't understand why you ask for him. Romeo, be careful here."

"May I speak to you in private?" the nurse asked Romeo.

Romeo extended his hand and led her down the street. They were buried by the townspeople, and their words were lost in the wind.

"Mercutio, don't follow him," Benvolio said. "He's in no danger. She's probably inviting him to supper. Stand back, unless you want to be forced to eat with her."

"Eat with her! She is too much, Benvolio. She is a rabbit. We shall hunt her, not dine with her, so let's go help Romeo."

"Leave them alone. Forget about her," Benvolio said.

Mercutio began to sing and dance, then suddenly stopped, defeated. "Too late. She made me hungry." He yelled after Romeo, "Romeo? Will you come to your father's with me for dinner?"

"Yes," Romeo hollered back. "I'll be right behind you." He brushed them away.

"Well then, good-bye, ancient lady, lady, lady, lady." Mercutio turned to Balthazar. "All right, Balthazar, come and find me food. Your man doesn't need you now. He has Peter and his wench."

"Great," Balthazar said, giving Benvolio a look. "Come with us then."

"I'll meet you there," Benvolio said. "Go on without me. I have something I need to do."

9

Benvolio made his way across the crowded street to the church. Mercutio and Balthazar left without question, and Romeo was deep in conversation with the nurse. Benvolio had managed to keep Romeo away from Tybalt, and soon the wedding would take place. Now he had to get to Rosaline and tell her everything that happened between Romeo and Juliet.

A lifetime of growing up in the church with a friend like Mercutio was a great benefit to help him get to Rosaline. Slowly Benvolio snuck around to the back of the church and crawled in through the cellar doors. He made his way through the dark basement and up the stone stairs. As children, they would sneak into the nuns' chambers to play tricks on them. He was a bit too big to fit through the small opening behind the draperies and statues now, but he found his way to Rosaline.

Emily Whitaker

She was standing alone beside a statue of the Virgin Mary. Rosaline's skin was as white as the statue's marble. He slipped behind the base of the Virgin Mary and looked around for anyone else, but they were alone.

"Rose," he whispered.

With a start, she turned. "Benvolio?" she whispered back.

He reached his arm to her and pulled her behind the statue.

"How did you get in here?" she asked.

"I had to come see you. I had to tell you what happened. I had to give you hope."

"Benvolio, my mother is talking to Sister Mary Margaret right now just around the corner."

"Listen to me, Rosaline. Last night, Romeo went to Juliet's balcony."

"He did what?"

"I followed and watched him climb her garden wall. I listened to her tell him she loves him, and he said he loves her."

"How did he? Wait, didn't she scream? Was he caught?"

"She was startled, but no one screams at Romeo. I mean, he's Romeo."

"Right."

"And it gets better. They made a plan to get married."

"Romeo and my cousin are planning to marry." She took his hand and kissed him on the cheek. "Benvolio, I have loved you from the moment you ran after me to make sure I was all right."

"You have?" he said.

"But from that moment, I have not forgotten that my love for you can never be more than our stolen time in the woods. They want to marry each other. So do we, but a Capulet will never marry a Montague. By becoming a nun and living in here, I can hold on to my love for you without the pain of pretending to love another man. This will always be the closest I can come to a happy end—"

Benvolio stopped her with a kiss. He held her as close to him as he could, breathing in the smell of her hair. "You didn't let me finish telling you everything," he said. "Last night, their plan to marry was for today. The moment Romeo left the Capulet villa, he came here to meet with Friar Lawrence. And this morning, after you came in here, Juliet's nurse met with Romeo to find out the time and place of the wedding. It's set, and they have both been true to their word. They will be married today."

"I don't believe it, Benvolio. Is that true? This is amazing news, too amazing. If my uncle is allowing this union, and so quickly, then we—"

"I'm sorry, Rosaline. Wait, I didn't mean…that's not the case. Your uncle doesn't know they're getting married today."

"I don't understand. Juliet will marry Romeo in secret? Benvolio, this doesn't change anything."

"Yes, it does. This will change everything for us."

"Then why don't we marry in secret right now?" she asked.

"I—"

An angry voice pierced the hall. "Rosaline, come here," her mother said.

"She is why," Benvolio said, holding Rosaline so she would stay with him. "Because you want it all, and I want to marry you in front of your mother and family. Believe in me, Rosaline, this plan will work."

"Rosaline, come now," her mother called.

Rosaline looked at Benvolio, and a beautiful smile filled her face. "I do, Benvolio. I do believe in you."

He let her go, and she went to her mother's side.

"Come, girl, they will take us to your quarters," her mother said.

The familiar pain of having to give Rosaline back to her mother killed him. Benvolio secretly followed them to Rosaline's quarters. He watched from an abandoned stairwell as she entered a small cold room.

"You won't be here long, my love," he whispered.

In the doorway, Rosaline paused, and he could see her smile.

"Did you hear that?" her mother said. "Old walls creaking, I suppose."

The three ladies entered the small dark room and shut the door behind them. Benvolio turned and made his way out of the church. Stepping into the heat of the bright sun, he sucked up the warmth and turned to go home.

10

Knowing Mercutio and Balthazar would be in the kitchen, Benvolio headed that way. He couldn't get his mind off the wedding. He knew that if Rosaline could witness it, she would see Romeo and Juliet's love was powerful enough to change everything.

"At last you've arrived," Mercutio said. He had taken a seat at the center of the busy kitchen. "Come, Benvolio, we will find a friendly place to feast. I'm starving." He glared at the help moving through the kitchen, as if they failed to understand that his choice of seating meant he should have been served.

"Where is Romeo?" Benvolio asked.

"He came a moment ago," Mercutio said. "He handed Balthazar a rope and told him to make it into a ladder and deliver it to that shameless, beetleheaded horn beast of a nurse in the town square. Then they both took off. Romeo said he had to give tithe at church. I yelled to him that he needed to feed me, but he didn't seem to care. Listen to me, Benvolio, I'm starving. I need to eat."

"Already?"

"What do you mean, already? I've been telling you that I'm starving for hours now."

"It's already happening?"

"What's already happening?"

"I'm sorry, Mercutio, but I have to go."

"Are you joking with me right now? Benvolio! Are you seriously not going to feed me?"

But Benvolio was already racing toward town. When he arrived at the church, Rosaline's mother was leaving, pretending to cry. He slid to a stop and jumped into the crowd to dodge her. He ran around to the side of the church, but he saw Romeo walking proudly through the side door. So Benvolio kept running to enter through the cellar again. He headed straight to Rosaline's room, hoping he could find her there, and he did. She was draped in black-and-white clothing, her hair modestly down around her shoulders. He felt pain in seeing Rosaline with her hair down. It was a stolen sight that only he was allowed to witness in the woods. It was a vision he held very close to his heart, and now all the people in the church would see the same thing.

"Rose," he whispered.

Startled, she turned. "Benvolio, why are you back here so soon?"

"It's time. Romeo and Juliet are getting married right now. Come with me to watch it. Please, Rosaline," he said, offering his hand.

"Benvolio, I'm supposed to pray by my bedside until someone comes to retrieve me."

"Right. Well, here I am to retrieve you. Come on, this is real. It's happening now, and it can change everything, secret or not. They are getting married in the church by Friar Lawrence. I mean, think about it. Not even your uncle can deny they are married once their union is sealed by God."

"I…well, that's true. Fine. I'll come with you, but I—"

He reached out and pulled her to follow him through the bowels of the church and down a tunnel until they hit the friar's chapel.

※

"I want Romeo to know that we are here for them," Benvolio said as they looked on from behind a pillar. "I want him to know that I believe in them and their love."

"I always imagined that I would be in Juliet's wedding. Wow, she looks beautiful. Are they really doing this?"

"They are. Let's go join them, stand beside them."

"Benvolio, I know what Romeo means to you, but this is a delicate moment. We shouldn't interrupt it. Let's just stand here, and together we are standing up for them at their wedding. When the time comes and Romeo says that he wishes you were there to share that moment with him, you can tell him that you were. How you stood up for your cousin because you believed in his love."

Benvolio took her hand. Quietly they listened to the words of love exchanged between their cousins and watched as those words were sealed with a kiss.

"So beautiful," Rosaline whispered. "We need to help them tell their fathers."

"I will get Romeo to tell me, and I will help him tell my uncle."

"I will speak to the friar and push him to tell my uncle with Juliet."

"This is the beginning, Rose. Your eyes are green."

She smiled.

11

The sun was hot and blinding in the late afternoon as Benvolio crawled out of the church cellar. He looked into the sycamore grove and took a deep breath. His desire to go back to those careless nights in the woods now had the hope of becoming a lifetime together. The sun bounced blue off a bundle of blooming flowers. Sicilian honey lilies were growing at the edge of the grove. Rosaline always picked them on her way home. Benvolio asked her once why she loved them, and she told him that they were the most beautiful flowers in the woods. She told him no one ever sold them because of their smell, so she was the only one who was able to truly enjoy their beauty. She also loved how they filled her room with the smell of garlic, making her mother go mad trying to find the source.

Benvolio gathered a bundle of the beautiful blue bulbs. He tore off the loose leather strap on his boot and tied the flowers together. He smelled them as she always did, and his head flew back. Their smell was overwhelming. He smiled and turned to crawl back into the cellar. He made his way to her drab box of a room, and it was empty. Her bed was made properly with a gray wool blanket pulled up over the flat pillow. There was a simple cross on the wall, a table beside her bed with a Bible on it, and a dresser in the corner with two drawers. There was one small window, high and stained with dark colors, letting in a little light. Benvolio looked around for the perfect place to leave the flowers. He wanted to display them for her, but he didn't want them to be taken away if found by someone else. He put them on top of the dresser. He stepped back to take a better look. The small room was already filling with the smell of garlic.

The church bells began to ring. Benvolio didn't need to count them to know what time it was. He needed to get to Mercutio and Balthazar before Romeo. He turned and left.

～

"What the hell, Benvolio," Mercutio yelled. "Where do you keep running off to, man?"

Benvolio took a seat beside Mercutio in the mist of the fountain.

"Chores," Benvolio answered.

"Chores at the church? While your servant has spent most of the day with me—doing nothing, I might add."

Balthazar looked a little irritated.

"It is time for a drink then," Benvolio said to ease the tension.

"I will go get wine," Balthazar said. "I've had enough of him, and I could use the air." He disappeared into the closest tavern.

"He's bringing some wine back for us, right?" Mercutio asked.

Benvolio turned to Mercutio. "I'm sorry about today and last night. Rosaline joined the nunnery this morning."

"I know. You keep sneaking in and out of that damn cellar beneath the church. Yes, I noticed. Did you think I didn't know what you were up to all day?"

"What did you tell Balthazar I was doing?"

"Do I owe an explanation to the help? No, I did not speak to your man unless I needed some wine, and in case you haven't noticed, I have no wine, so it has been a very tough day for me."

"I'm sure it has been."

"Is Rosaline going to be all right in there?"

"She's living in a stone-cold room with no candles, a small window, and one scratchy gray blanket, Mercutio. I could break her out, you know?"

"Then do it."

"I can't. I'm not the only person in this world who is lucky enough to be loved by her. She cares about her mother. I can see it in her eyes when she talks about her.

Emily Whitaker

No, I can't do it, but I can hope to change this world we live in. Change the reason she's in there."

"Change it! Please, Benvolio, you would have better luck in a battle of wits with her mother."

"I can at least hope to find a way to end this fight."

"Impossible."

"Why is it?"

"This fight is a fire inside all of us. You are filled with love and peace and whatever, and because of that, you have never understood this fight. The same goes for Romeo, and it's a quality I tolerate in both of you. However, the truth is, this fire has been fueled for many years by hate. Hate that no one can tell you where it started or how it started, only that it's strong and raging. Tell me, Benvolio, have you ever put out a fire?"

"Well, I have—"

"Have you ever put out a raging fire using nothing but peace and love and poetry?"

"I believe my uncle is tired and wants this fight to end. I believe Lord Capulet feels the same, and so does your cousin the prince."

"It is a heavy burden to put on old men, to change how they have always thought, what they have always believed in."

"At the party last night, I heard Lord Capulet say to Tybalt that he wanted to find peace with us. He demanded that Tybalt let Romeo enjoy the party in his home."

"And now Tybalt has challenged Romeo to a duel. How did he send his challenge? Oh yes, with a letter sealed with the Capulet crest. Don't you see that old man Capulet only wanted to stop his nephew from ruining his party? I'm sure he sent Tybalt to fight Romeo this morning."

Balthazar returned with their wine. "Speaking of Tybalt," he said. He pointed down the street, put their wine on the edge of the fountain, and quickly drank what was left of his. Then he took a fighting stance with one hand on his sword.

"Listen to me," Benvolio said. "Romeo has been doing something very important today. I never got a chance to tell him that Tybalt has challenged him. Did either of you?"

Balthazar shook his head.

"He has been doing something very important with a rope ladder?" Mercutio asked.

Benvolio replied, "Well, yes, but listen. We can't let him fight Tybalt. We have to find Romeo and bring him home. It's hot out, and I know you want to see Tybalt brought to his knees, Mercutio. I know you always do. And I assume Tybalt is just as hot to fight. But we have to find Romeo before Tybalt does. Whatever you do, Mercutio, do not fight him."

Trying to look calm, Benvolio took a stance, keeping his eye on Tybalt.

Mercutio rolled his eyes and began circling him and said, "Jesus, Benvolio, you are like one of these men who enter a tavern and draw their sword just to put it on the table as they ask God to give them no need to fight. Then, after a drink or two, they draw their sword from the table and threaten the waiter with it. So don't speak to me of hot tempers."

"Really, Mercutio? That is who I am?"

Mercutio backed away from him dramatically. "Settle down, Benvolio. You are a wild man when you are moody, as any Italian man is. You are easily pushed into a rage. You are a huge fighter."

"Oh, I am? What a change in opinion, Mercutio," Benvolio said, irritated and trying not to lose sight of Tybalt. "To what end do I fight?"

"I have seen you start fights with men who have a hair less, or a hair more, on their chin than you. If a man cracks a nut, you fight him, and for no other reason but because you have hazel eyes. Who but your hazel eyes would seek out such a fight?"

"What are you talking about, Mercutio? My eyes are brown," Benvolio said.

"Don't you see, Benvolio?" Balthazar said. "He's pushing your buttons. He's pushing you to fight. We're hot. We're tired. You're right. We need to find Romeo and go home."

"For the love of God, I am so hungry," Mercutio yelled. "Make your man go get me some food."

"That's enough, Mercutio," Benvolio said. "Keep your eyes on Tybalt. He's coming this way."

"Your mind is as obsessed with fighting as an egg is full of meat," Mercutio said. "And yet it's your head that has been beaten like an egg for fighting. You once fought with a man who coughed on the street because he woke your dog, who was sleeping in the sun."

"Mercutio, relax." Benvolio picked up his wine. "Here, drink this. It will calm you down."

Mercutio drank it in one gulp. "And was it not you," he said, spitting wine as he spoke, "who fought with your tailor for wearing his tight new jacket before Easter? Oh, and the fight you had with the man who tied his new shoes with old ribbon? And yet you stand here and think you can tell me not to fight?"

"Mercutio, I am a peaceful man, as you said yourself. If you are saying that I'm as ready to fight as you are, then every man here should buy my temper for one hour and only for one quarter. Because I am calm, and I'm not going to fight. And neither are you."

"Easier said than done, Benvolio." Mercutio took the other glass of wine and downed it as well.

Benvolio had not lost track of Tybalt as he passed through the crowd. He watched his every move as Mercutio ranted on. "All right, he saw us, and now he's coming our way," Benvolio said, looking around for Romeo.

"Seriously, who cares?" Mercutio said.

Tybalt moved in front of Benvolio with an army of men behind him.

"Follow me closely, men. I'll be speaking to a Montague." Then he addressed Benvolio's lot, "Gentlemen, good afternoon. A word with one of you."

Mercutio stepped between them, getting in Tybalt's face. "Just one word with one of us?" Mercutio mocked. "Make it more interesting than that. Perhaps sing your word or blow it."

"You will find me ready to strike and blow, sir, and I'm sure you will give me reason to do so," Tybalt replied.

"Can you not hear a joke without wanting to kill a man, Tybalt?"

"Mercutio, you are friends with Romeo. You consort with him?"

"Consort? I consort with him? Do you think we are musicians? Do you hear nothing but angry music when I speak to you? Oh, look. Here is my fiddlestick. I'll use it to make you dance. Jesus, man. Yes, I consort with Romeo." Mercutio happily invaded Tybalt's space as he spoke.

"Gentlemen," Benvolio said, stepping in. "We are talking here in the public square among men. We should either go somewhere private to talk this out or let us all go our separate ways. But here all the men of Verona can see what we're doing. And there is one man I don't want to join us."

"Man's eyes are meant to look upon action," Mercutio said. "I say, let them watch. I won't walk away."

"Well," Tybalt said with a smile. "I won't engage in this action with such scum as you. Anyway, here comes my man."

Romeo was walking toward them. Benvolio stepped toward Tybalt, but before he could say a word, Mercutio grabbed Benvolio's arm and pushed him away.

"Let me try to outwit him, Benvolio. Trust me. Maybe it will take his mind off Romeo." Mercutio stepped toward Tybalt. "I swear, I'll just die if Romeo has become one of your servants. No, it can't be, I know it. Listen, Tybalt. We will go to a field where we can fight, but Romeo doesn't fight, you see. So perhaps he only followed you here in worship because that's the only way that you can call him your man."

"Romeo," Tybalt called out past Mercutio. "The love I have for you can be expressed with a name: villain, Romeo. You are a villain."

Mercutio looked at Benvolio. "I'm trying, I truly am, but if you don't want him to fight Romeo, then I have to fight him myself."

"No, I think we should let Romeo speak. He will prove to you that his love can stop all of this," Benvolio answered.

Mercutio didn't leave his place between Romeo and Tybalt.

"Tybalt," Romeo said. "The reason I have to love you is greater than your hate for me. I am no villain, so please, let's go our separate ways. It is clear you do not know what kind of man I am."

"Boy," Tybalt said, stepping to him and trying to get around Mercutio. "Your little speech does not excuse what you've done to me. You must turn and fight me."

"Tybalt, I don't believe I have done anything wrong to you. You must understand that I love you better than you can know. Until you realize the reason for my love toward you, good Capulet, which is a name I hold as dearly as my own, I will not fight you."

Tybalt took another step toward Romeo and reached for his sword. Mercutio pushed Romeo out of the away.

"Oh, enough with the calm words, Romeo," Mercutio said. "You bring dishonor to your family with your pathetic words of love. Alla staccato, the fencing cat Tybalt, will you walk without a fight?" Mercutio grabbed the butt of his sword with excitement, dancing in front of Tybalt like a string to a cat. He whispered over his shoulder, "Move away, Romeo."

"Why do you want to fight me?" Tybalt asked.

"Good king of cats, I would like nothing more than to take one of your nine lives and, perhaps, the other eight as well. Will you draw your sword from its leather? You better hurry, Tybalt. My sword will be slicing around your ears by the time you draw."

Benvolio grabbed Romeo and pulled him away.

"I'll fight you," Tybalt said, drawing his sword.

Romeo pulled his arm out of Benvolio's grip. "Gentle Mercutio, put your sword away," he said.

"Come, Tybalt, show me your moves," Mercutio said.

Romeo turned back to Benvolio. "Draw, Benvolio," Romeo said. "Make them put down their weapons."

"You were right when you told me it was wrong to draw my sword to keep the peace. Let them do what they will. Come home with me now to your father and leave them to themselves. Please, Romeo, come with me. You know what is at stake," Benvolio replied.

Romeo drew his sword. "You don't understand, Benvolio. I can't let them hurt each other. I do know what is at stake. It's you who doesn't understand."

"Tell me, Romeo, tell me everything. Tell me why staying out of this fight is not what is best."

Romeo looked to the ground and then up to the heavens. Then he turned toward the fight with his sword in the air. "Gentlemen, stop this fight at once!" he called. "Tybalt, Mercutio, listen to me!" Romeo ran after them as they fought, circling them, trying to get their attention. "The prince expressly forbids us to fight in the streets of Verona. The punishment is death. Stop, Tybalt!"

Benvolio tried to pull Romeo out of the way but couldn't get to him. Romeo pushed himself into the fight to make them stop. He took his stand in front of Mercutio, facing Tybalt eye to eye, but Tybalt did not stop his sword. With a lunging thrust, Tybalt's hot blade slid under Romeo's arm.

"Good Mercutio," Romeo said, turning to him.

Mercutio had fallen to the ground. Benvolio rushed to him as Tybalt and his men walked away.

"I'm hurt," Mercutio said. "I curse a plague on both your houses. Your fight has ended me. Is he gone? Tybalt, you coward, you ran without a scratch."

Benvolio could see the wound through Mercutio's thin white shirt. The blood was overwhelming. "What's wrong?" Benvolio said lightly, trying not to worry him. "What, man, are you hurt?"

"No, it's only a scratch. It's nothing. Where is that wretched serving man?"

Balthazar came to Mercutio.

"Go and bring me back a surgeon," Mercutio ordered.

Balthazar took off running.

"Have some courage. It can't be that bad," Romeo said.

"No," Mercutio said, his voice starting to crack. "My wound is not deep like a well or wide like a church door, but it's enough. Ask for me tomorrow, and you will find me in a grave. I'm done with this world. A plague on both your houses! Leave it to a cat like Tybalt to scratch a man to death and to do it by the fencing manual. Why the devil did you come between us, Romeo? I was hurt under your arm."

"I was trying to stop you. I thought I was doing the right thing."

Mercutio grabbed Benvolio's hand.

"Help me inside, Benvolio, or I'll faint. A plague on both your houses. They have buried me in the ground to be eaten by worms. You have taken my life. I'll curse your houses."

Benvolio pulled Mercutio into a tavern. The moment they entered, a large woman scooped up Mercutio and brought him into a room in the back. She gently placed him on the bed as she swiped away a tear.

"I'll go get Signor Mercutio some brandy," she said as she disappeared into the bar area.

"Ah, where is that surgeon?" Mercutio asked.

"Rest, he's coming. Move your hand and let me take a look," Benvolio said.

When Mercutio moved his hand, the blood poured out. Benvolio grabbed his handkerchief and pushed against the wound to stop the bleeding. The large woman returned. She handed Mercutio a bottle of brandy and began to tear his shirt at the seam. Teardrops were falling from her eyes onto his chest.

"Move your hand, young man. Only for a moment," she said.

Benvolio took his hand away from Mercutio's wound, bringing the cloth off with him. The woman poured vodka onto the gash, washing the blood away and leaving a small hole that had clearly sliced his side. Mercutio was in pain, and his face turned from a pale white to gray. The woman handed Benvolio a clean rag.

"Use this to keep the pressure on the wound," she said.

"My life," Mercutio said. "Your pathetic fight has taken my life, and for what? Benvolio, for what? Find me one man, a Montague or a Capulet, who can tell me before I die what they are fighting for. Aye, a plague on both your houses."

"Enough, Mercutio," Benvolio said. "That fight was started by you."

"Oh, stop with your love and peace, Benvolio. Tybalt came looking for a fight, and better me than Romeo."

"Better no one. We could have left."

"I'll never walk away from such a man as Tybalt."

"And why not? You don't respect Tybalt, so why honor him with a fight? You said yourself you don't understand this fight. So why do you fuel it with your hate for a man like Tybalt?"

"The man just took my life, Benvolio. Don't take away my hate for him. Besides, don't you understand what this means? My death will be the end of Tybalt. The Montagues have won."

"No, we haven't won, Mercutio. You're the one who doesn't understand. There can't be a winner in a fight like this. Your death won't end this fight. The prince can't end it with his words or by anything rational, like punishing Tybalt. Not when it's so out of control. The only thing strong enough to stop this is our love. We need to learn to love one another."

"Oh, enough, man. Come on. Never has your love for Rosaline made a dent in this world. Now that you know she loves you back, you think that will change things?"

"You're right, but a love between Romeo and Capulet's daughter, Juliet, might."

"Am I hallucinating? What did she give me to drink?" He took another swig. "What is your plan here, Ben? Romeo might fall in love with everything that dances, but Juliet Capulet? Well, it doesn't matter whether her heart would land with Romeo. She is promised to my cousin Paris, cousin to the prince as well."

"Wait, she's promised to Paris?"

"He is still in discussions with her father. Nothing has been made official, but he has been bragging how he will have her hand."

"It doesn't matter," Benvolio said. "Look at me. Listen to me. I witnessed the marriage of Romeo and Juliet myself this morning in the friar's chapel. Their love is real, and they are united under the eyes of God. It is strong enough."

"I don't understand." He flinched in pain, and Benvolio helped him take another swig of brandy.

"Last night—"

"No, I'm dying, you fool. I have no time for details. You tell me the truth? They are married?"

"They are."

"The son of Montague has married the daughter of Capulet in secret?"

"They have."

"Why didn't you tell me, Benvolio? I drew my sword against an enemy today and gave him my life. Would I have drawn my sword if I had known about this union?"

"I don't—"

"I would hope that I would not. Romeo and Juliet are married. Oh, Benvolio, the pain is too much."

"Hold on, man. The surgeon is on his way. Drink."

Benvolio could feel Mercutio's body tense against the pain.

"How was the wedding?" Mercutio asked.

"It was peaceful and full of love."

"If it's their love that ends this fight, it won't be easy."

"I know."

"Of course, you know. That's why you never had the codpiece to do it yourself. Oh, come on, look at me. Do not leave this up to Romeo. Don't let him fight this alone. You have to help him. If he is not ready to tell us about his secret love, help him some other way, but always be there. When that boy has to face Lord Capulet, he will need strength. He will need you by his side."

Mercutio began to cough. Blood escaped through his lungs and stomach, flooding his mouth and nose.

"Drink," was all Benvolio could think to say.

"Drink with me. To Romeo and Juliet, may they live long and happy lives together." He gasped for breath.

Benvolio took a drink and poured some in Mercutio's mouth.

"May their love spread like water through the fiery hearts of angry men," Mercutio continued. They drank. "And may my actions today, and my death, only serve as a reminder never to return to the hate that once ran their lives."

They drank. Mercutio grabbed the bottle from Benvolio and began to chug it. He coughed, and his skin turned a clammy yellow. The pillow propping up his head was soaked with sweat. Benvolio looked at the wound. The rag was dripping blood. He leaned in with more pressure.

"Benvolio, avenge my death with your silly love. I see it now. You were right all along," Mercutio said, smiling. His body relaxed into the bed. "The pain is not so bad anymore," he said.

The bottle slipped out of Mercutio's hand and rolled away from the bed.

"Mercutio?" Benvolio said softly.

Mercutio looked at him and smiled. His eyes shook, and his muscles clenched around the wound. Benvolio pushed against the wound tighter, fighting to keep Mercutio's life inside him, but he could feel Mercutio's pulse begin to slow.

"Mercutio, no. Please hold on a moment longer. Where is the surgeon?" he yelled. "Where the hell is the surgeon?"

The large woman was standing by the door. She bent down to pick up the bottle of brandy. When she stood, her eyes were wet, and she shook her head.

Benvolio turned to Mercutio. "Come on, man, wake up! Wake up, you damn fool."

Benvolio shook his body, but Mercutio didn't open his eyes. He leaned in and grabbed Mercutio's face and held it tightly against his as he spoke, "Listen to me, Mercutio. It's a scratch, that's all. You open your damn eyes now, and you come through this. I need you alive, man. I need you alive."

His tears mixed with Mercutio's sweat. Benvolio clenched his teeth and held his breath in an attempt to stop crying. In the silence, he heard a deep moan escape his friend. He felt his chest fall.

"He's gone, boy," the woman in the doorway said.

Benvolio collapsed beside Mercutio's bed. His hand fell away from the wound, leaving the bloody rag stuck to Mercutio's body. Benvolio cried into his bloody hands. The woman came to his side and offered him the bottle of brandy.

"He was my friend," he told her, taking the bottle.

She nodded and put her hand on his back.

"He was hungry," he continued. "He wanted us to go get food." He started to cry again. "Why didn't I just get him food? Why?" He looked at Mercutio's silent face and pushed himself away from the body until he hit the wall behind him. "No, no, no, no. This is not how today was supposed to end! Damn it, Mercutio."

The woman stepped away as Benvolio made it to his feet. He saw that his anger was scaring her, but he couldn't control it. He took a swig of the brandy and tossed the bottle. He stumbled out of the room into the dark bar and then into the bright hot street.

Romeo was where he had left him, his loving eyes filled with pain.

"Romeo," Benvolio called to him. "Romeo, Mercutio is dead."

As Benvolio said the words, the sounds of the street left his ears. The sun darkened to gray. His breath became focused. He moved forward, hunting the man who had killed his friend. "Tybalt is coming back, look," he told Romeo.

"Coming back with his life in triumph as Mercutio lies dead," Romeo yelled. "To hell with being the lover. I'm filled with nothing but hate now, and I'll let it lead me. Come to me, Tybalt. Take this hate from me that you've given me in a trade for Mercutio's soul, still close above our heads. He is waiting for you to keep him company in death. Maybe he is waiting for me, or both of us."

"You wretched boy, Romeo, you listen to me now," Tybalt said. "It is your fault your friend Mercutio is dead, and now you will join him."

"We will see about that," Romeo said.

Swords high, they lunged at each other. Benvolio stayed beside Romeo with his sword drawn. He wanted to jump in and take a wild swipe at Tybalt. He wanted to lunge toward him with the small tip of his sword. But he stood and waited for his moment, knowing better than to come between two men as they fought. He watched their every move. The swords clanked and slid as they ran and chased each other through the streets of Verona. Dust was building up around them as they twisted and lunged in anger. A stone wall pushed against Benvolio's back and forced him to look away from the fight. His back hit the church. The sun filled his eyes, and figures were yelling and running through the streets in front of him.

"Romeo, no," Benvolio screamed.

He realized what he was doing, that he had let his rage take control of him. As he ran toward Romeo, his screams were lost in the crowd's cheers and hollers. He tried to plow through the people, but they were too strong. He couldn't see Romeo, so he focused his ears on the sound of their swords. He followed it as their fight moved into the town square. A gasp from the crowd forced Benvolio to look up. Tybalt had taken the higher ground by jumping onto the ledge of the center fountain, swiping and scratching from above as he balanced on the fountain's edge. Benvolio couldn't see Romeo, but he saw Tybalt jump to avoid a blow to his legs. Then he saw Romeo pummel into Tybalt. A splash came from the fountain as they both fell in.

Benvolio jumped into the fountain to stop them. "Romeo, please stop this!" he yelled.

But Romeo had already stopped. The crowd was silent. Tybalt's body was floating peacefully with the waves in the fountain. A red cloud of blood was filling the water as Romeo's sword fell with a splash from his hand.

"Romeo," Benvolio whispered. He forced himself to move through the bloody water toward his cousin. "Romeo."

Benvolio grabbed Romeo's arm and turned him away from Tybalt's body. "Romeo, you have to leave. The people are starting to stir, and soon everyone will know that Tybalt has been killed. Romeo, look at me. You can't stand here any longer. You have to go. The prince will have your head if he finds you standing over Tybalt's dead body. I'll speak to him and see what I can do for you, but please, you must go now. Go! Run now!"

"What have I done, Benvolio? I acted like a puppet in a fight I don't even believe in."

They had both acted against themselves.

"Romeo, go now."

12

The crowd was too wild to notice that Romeo was leaving. Benvolio stepped out of the fountain.

"Benvolio," Balthazar said. He was sweaty and out of breath. "It is true."

Benvolio's heart lifted at the sight of a friend. "Will you help me?" he asked.

Balthazar climbed into the fountain, and together they carried Tybalt's body out, putting him gracefully on the ground. Benvolio pushed Balthazar into the crowd and stood over Tybalt's body alone. He listened as the crowd changed their wild hollers to civil mumblings. The prince stepped forward.

"Tell me who are the villains who began this fight today," the prince addressed the crowd.

Benvolio knelt and bowed. "Noble Prince, I can tell you everything about this terrible fight." His voice was breaking. He took a deep breath and began, "Here is Tybalt.

He has been killed by Romeo, who was taken by the pain after Tybalt killed Mercutio."

Benvolio paused. He understood that the news of the prince's kinsman Mercutio would hurt him as much as it hurt Romeo and himself. But before the prince could speak, a scream broke through the crowd.

"Tybalt, my cousin!" It was Juliet's mother, Lady Capulet.

The crowd parted to let her through. She fell onto Tybalt's lifeless wet body. As she cried out his name, the pain in her voice ripped through Benvolio. Any bit of hope that Romeo's life with Juliet could survive this tragedy was fading fast.

"Benvolio," the prince addressed him. "How did this happen?"

Benvolio stayed on one knee with his head hung low as he told the prince the dreadful actions of the afternoon, and as he spoke, he saw his faults. He heard Rosaline's warnings against Tybalt and could not make sense of his actions toward him.

"Yes, it's true that Romeo killed Tybalt. But that's not how it all began. It was Tybalt who came looking for a fight, and it was Romeo who would only give him kind words. Romeo didn't want to fight, but Tybalt would have none of Romeo's peace. Tybalt's fire was answered by Mercutio, not Romeo. Mercutio engaged in a fight, and Romeo tried again and again to stop them. But he could not break them up. So he put himself between them, hoping it would calm them down and bring them back to sanity. He was reminding them that you, Prince, warned against us fighting. But in that moment that was supposed to bring only peace, Tybalt stabbed Mercutio beneath Romeo's arm."

Benvolio held his breath. Speaking the words of Mercutio's death made him want to scream at Lady Capulet, who was still crying over Tybalt's dead body. He wanted to tell her that the monster beneath her deserved to die. He looked at Lady Capulet. Her head was down, and her dark gown resembled Rosaline's mother's exactly. He knew he needed to stay strong and not let the hatred engulf him again. He needed to do it for Rosaline, for Romeo, and for Juliet. He picked out a stone on the ground and focused on it, forcing the sight of his friend's lifeless body from his mind.

He began again. "Tybalt fled, but then he came back to us. He came back to us, and all we wanted was to mourn the death of our friend. Mercutio's soul had just left us, and our minds were fueled by rage and revenge. He was our closest friend, and his life was taken. In that moment, with our hearts on fire, Romeo and Tybalt fought like lightning. Before the fire in my heart could calm and know well enough to stop them, Tybalt was killed. As Tybalt fell, I told Romeo to leave so I could tell you the truth about this fight and make sure the fight between our families is not given any more fuel to grow from our ignorant actions. This is the truth, Prince, I swear on my life."

Lady Capulet cried out, "This boy is a Montague. His love for his family makes his story false."

Her words stabbed Benvolio. His love for her family had made not only his words but his foolish actions fill with more pain than she could ever imagine.

She screamed out as loud as she could, "Romeo has killed Tybalt! Romeo must die!"

The prince silenced the rustling crowd. "Romeo killed Tybalt! Tybalt killed Mercutio! Who is going to pay for Mercutio's death?"

"Not Romeo, Prince," Lord Montague said. He had joined the crowd, and Benvolio felt relief with his presence. "He was Mercutio's friend. Romeo killing Tybalt is what the law would have done, to take the life of the man who killed Mercutio. That is all."

"Exactly, Lord Montague," the prince said. "Romeo has taken a life, but so has Tybalt. To this end, I do exile Romeo from Verona. Do not fight me on this judgment. The blood spilled today is my blood too. Mercutio was my family, and I'll mourn him greatly. So I'll hold you to this exile, that all of you will understand the loss of this day. Do not bother to plead or give me your excuses, tears, or prayers. Nothing will change my mind on this. Make sure Romeo leaves immediately. If he does not and he tries to stay in Verona and I find him, that moment will be his last. Take this body from the streets and attend to the families. I'm showing mercy toward murderers and pardoning those who kill."

The prince shook his head and hung it low as he departed. The Capulet men took Tybalt's body away.

Tybalt's blood was wet in the sand beside Benvolio. Dust sat in the hot air, not yet settled from their fight. What happened to the love that filled the day with so much hope? It could have been seconds. It could have been hours that passed, but Benvolio never moved from his spot on the ground.

"Benvolio," a soft voice said.

His head spun. He looked to the spot where Tybalt's body had been. It was dry and stained until a bucket of steaming water was splashed on it. A figure with flowing black hair, in black and white robes, started to scrub the bloody spot.

"Benvolio," the figure whispered to him.

His eyes focused. It was Rosaline. Behind her stood two nuns working silently, draining the fountain to clean off the bloodstained tiles.

"Rose?" he whispered. "Why are you here on the streets? They aren't safe."

"They sent us here to clean up the spilled blood," she told him.

"Do you know what happened here?"

"I do, Benvolio."

"I have ruined everything." His face fell into his hands to hide the tears. "This rage grew inside me, Rosaline, and I don't understand why. He asked me to keep the peace."

Benvolio

He looked at her. "He believed that their love could end this fight, and his death would not have been in vain. But once his soul left his body, all peace left my mind. I did this, Rosaline. I have killed all of our hope."

"You have not. My aunt and uncle came to the church with Tybalt's body. My aunt was screaming and crying desperately, and my uncle was just standing there. I heard him tell Friar Lawrence that Tybalt's death was a relief. And then he just watched my aunt, so confused by her pain."

"It doesn't change the fact that a Montague killed a Capulet today."

"No, but it also doesn't change the fact that our cousins are bound in marriage. Two men are dead today, and both of our families are in no condition to change their minds about one another. But soon they will find out about Romeo and Juliet, and they will have to at least try. Tonight there's nothing more that can be done except be supportive to our grieving families. Your cousin is banished. My cousin's new husband is banished. What you need to do now is go home. Be with your aunt and uncle and help them grieve their banished son. Our time will come."

"This is all on my bloody hands," he said.

She took his hands. "They are only covered in tears, Benvolio. Listen to me. Right after Romeo killed Tybalt, he came to find shelter at the friar's. I was supposed to be taking prayer, but I could hear him crying. I knew his voice, and I could tell something had gone wrong. I tried to listen to what he was telling the friar, and then I heard the voice of my cousin's nurse, a voice I could never miss. And suddenly Romeo's pain was gone. I couldn't tell what was going on, so I snuck closer to get a better look. Romeo's face was still sunken with guilt, but his eyes were full of hope. Then he left the friar's with Juliet's nurse."

"It is his wedding night. I should have expected he would spend it with Juliet."

"It is her cousin's blood that I'm cleaning from the streets, put there by her new husband. It is all so much to understand."

"Rosaline, Romeo is banished for what he has done here. He can't spend the night with his stolen bride now."

"I know, but I believe that tonight Romeo must be with his wife. It is not a joy that should be taken from either of them."

"And tomorrow he flees this place, and we will be left to bury our loved ones alone."

"Don't hate Romeo for loving his wife tonight, Benvolio."

"Mercutio is dead, and Romeo has killed a man. And you, why don't you hate me right now?"

"For the same reason Juliet is letting the man who killed her cousin into her bed tonight. I love you, but I have always understood the world I live in. This hate our families have for one another is deeper than skin. It is in our blood. I have seen it boil, and I always knew it was strong. When Tybalt came back into town, when Romeo came to my home to profess his love for me, it was only a matter of time before blood was spilled. I've always known this would happen, and I have always loved you anyway. Don't give up, Benvolio. Don't question us."

Benvolio reached for Rosaline's face. Her cheeks were as pink as the sun setting behind her. He could see the hope still alive within her.

"Benvolio, I love you."

"I love you, Rosaline." He pulled her toward him and kissed her. His chapped lips melted at the soft touch of hers. His hand found her waist, and he pulled her even closer. She wrapped her hands around his neck and held tightly to him. Sister Mary Margaret came close to them and cleared her throat.

Benvolio reluctantly let her go. "What am I supposed to do now?" he asked.

"Tonight Romeo celebrates his marriage, but tomorrow he has to leave this place. You need to go home. Be with your aunt and uncle. Go now. Keep off the streets and be where you are needed most."

13

Benvolio got to his feet. With one last look at Rosaline, he began to walk home. How could he be of any comfort to his aunt and uncle when he felt so weak? He was the cause of everything that had gone wrong in the day. If he had kept Romeo calm, the prince would be banishing Tybalt. Or better, he would sentence him to a rightful death, leaving Romeo free to love his wife in peace. Now Romeo was lying with the cousin of the man he killed, and Benvolio was left alone to bury Mercutio and comfort Romeo's parents. His heart was pounding. He felt dizzy and sick. He sank to the ground as people hustled around him.

"It is a tragic night for the Capulets," Benvolio heard a man in the crowd say.

"I suppose this means your wedding to Juliet Capulet is off."

"Tybalt, their nephew, is dead," another man said. "And then Mercutio was a dear friend to them. The loss of this day won't be forgotten anytime soon."

Benvolio looked up. It was Paris.

"No, it won't be forgotten, but the wedding is going to happen," Paris continued. "Her father is a wise man and understands the beauty of love. Two people brought together in marriage will have the strength to bring peace to grieving hearts."

Benvolio stood and moved into the shadows. The sun had set, and he was able to hide completely in the dark. He couldn't let Paris see how sick he was at his announcement.

"But, Paris, do you truly want to marry into a family with such turmoil?" one of the men asked.

"The fight between the Capulets and Montagues is ancient. But Juliet's father and I agree it has to end with his generation. Now that there is death on each family's hands, my kinsman, the prince, will stand for none of it. My marriage into the Capulet family will bring an end to this fight. This night will be the last of Juliet's pain."

"And when will you marry the young Juliet?"

"This Thursday."

Benvolio fell against the wall behind him.

"So soon?" a man asked.

"When a powerful man like Lord Capulet can find peace in such a dark time, you follow," Paris said.

"And the Lady Juliet? She isn't taking time to be in mourning for her cousin?"

"Her father is giving her time to mourn tonight. He will tell her of our marriage tomorrow in hopes that her heart will heal with our love and the excitement of our wedding. It is what the town and the Capulets need. This fight has gone on long enough, and today will be the last of it."

"Well, then, come on. I'll buy you a drink. To Paris and Juliet. Oh, I like the way that sounds."

Benvolio wanted to do something, but he could hear Rosaline's voice telling him to go home. So he started to walk. His head was down, and his feet led him. Lord Capulet wanted peace and felt a wedding would bring it? If only that wedding could have been Romeo and Juliet's. Benvolio could see Mercutio's face fall again in his mind. The water was rushing around him, red with Tybalt's blood, a dull sword slicing his cheek. He fell to the ground, and the earth soaked through to his hot back, cooling his skin and calming him. His eyes focused on the swaying tree branch that had cut his face. Beyond the branch, the stars came into focus.

He wasn't shocked to find that his feet had carried him to the sycamore grove. He stayed lying in the dirt until his heart found a steady rhythm. The day of blood was behind him, and the events were finally becoming clear. They were no longer blurred with loss and rage. He couldn't change what he had done, but the news of Juliet's wedding to Paris could cause Romeo to act out of anger again. He needed to get to his cousin. He needed to be strong for him this time and make sure Romeo left safely to Mantua.

The stars were fading in the new light of the rising sun. He had been on the ground all night. Even the lark was awake and singing loudly. He needed to get to Romeo. He got up and wiped the dirt from his clothes. He dabbed at his bloody cheek with his sleeve. The cut was no longer bleeding, but singed at his touch. He buttoned his shirt and straightened his collar. As he began to walk toward the Capulet villa, he pulled down his sleeves until he saw Tybalt's blood had dyed them red. He rolled them back up, tucked in his shirt, and brushed his fingers through his hair.

Dew was collecting on the leaves, and a sweet mist was filling the air as the sun quickly rose. Benvolio made his way down along the Capulet wall to the reaching trees. He climbed into the Capulet yard and ran to Juliet's private garden. When he arrived, he wasn't sure what to do. He turned to wait and saw the sun had taken its place in the sky. It was getting late. Romeo needed to get out of there and out of Verona. Benvolio turned and climbed Juliet's garden wall. He could see two figures moving in Juliet's chambers. He climbed the vines beside her balcony as Romeo had done. And when he got to her balcony, he could hear the voice of Juliet's mother, filled with rage.

"Don't speak to me, child. I have nothing left to say to you. I'm done with you."

He heard a door slam, and he went to climb onto the balcony. He was sure Romeo and Juliet had been caught, but then he heard Juliet cry out.

"Oh God, Nurse, how do I save my marriage to Romeo now? He has left to be banished to Mantua. He's not dead, and now I'm engaged to marry Paris. What am I supposed to do? Do you have any idea how to help me with this?"

Romeo was already gone, and Juliet's mourning time had apparently ended. Benvolio needed to find Romeo before anyone else had the chance. But Juliet's words pierced through the garden, and her pain at the prospect of marrying Paris gave him hope. She didn't want to follow her father's orders. He decided to stay and listen, hoping to hear the nurse's plan. Perhaps he could help them and make peace of this mess.

"I do have a way to help you, my dear child," the nurse said. "Juliet, your Romeo is banished. He can't come to your bed ever again without the penalty of death. This is the wicked truth, my dear. So, as it stands, I believe you should forget him and marry Paris. Besides, Paris is a better match for you than Romeo. He is handsomer, richer, and by far, a better man to love you."

"Do you really think that I should marry Paris?" Juliet asked.

"No," Benvolio whispered.

"I do," the nurse said.

"Amen," Juliet said.

"What, my child?"

"Nurse, you have comforted me greatly. Please go tell my mother that I have left to go to Friar Lawrence's cell to pray for forgiveness for upsetting my father. I'll pray to be absolved of all my sins."

"Oh, you've come around to see the joy in this second marriage. I'll go tell your mother now."

Benvolio ran out of her garden. Sick with fury, he climbed the wall and ran out of the Capulet yard. He ran down the wall's outer edge and through the town to his uncle's home. He had to find Romeo. He didn't know what he was going to say to him, but he had to make sure no one else had the chance to tell him first.

As he arrived at his uncle's, he saw the villa's staff and his aunt and uncle standing out front, waving away a carriage that was disappearing over the far-off hillside. He had missed Romeo. He stood there breathing deeply, not willing to approach his aunt and uncle. He could see that his aunt was white with loss; her tears had taken over her sweet face. His uncle was standing tall beside her, using every muscle in his body and mind to do as the prince had told him: to believe that the banishment of his son was a kind of justice. Benvolio knew what this meant to his uncle. Not only would he be consumed by the pain of never having his son in his home again but of the fact that his home was meant to eventually be Romeo's home. His hills of olives and grapevines were meant to be Romeo's hills.

Romeo's life, as it was known, was over, though his heart was still beating in his chest.

As the carriage disappeared completely, Benvolio saw his aunt fall to her knees. His uncle shouted at the help to leave them alone. He lifted his wife and carried her into their home, leaving everyone standing outside. The door shut behind him, but still Benvolio did not move. He couldn't grieve with his aunt and uncle; he didn't want to. He wished he were still lying on the cool dirt alone in the woods. He turned and started to walk toward town. Again his feet knew where to take him. He looked up at the church and didn't know if he had come there to fall into Rosaline's arms and never leave them or to seek the friar for help in figuring out what he was supposed to do next.

He was stepping forward to go through the front doors of the church when the doors opened in front of him. Paris stepped out with a smile on his face. Benvolio put his head down and walked into the church around Paris. He ran to the friar's chambers, but he stopped when he heard Juliet's voice. He peeked through a crack in the door. Juliet was weeping.

"Oh, shut the door," she said. "And then come cry with me. There is no hope, no care, and no help for me."

The friar shut the door, and Benvolio listened through the cracks in the doorway.

"Oh, Juliet, I already know why you are grieving, and it's killing me as well. I know that you're going to be married on Thursday to Paris, and that nothing can be done to stop it."

"Oh, thank you, Juliet," Benvolio whispered to himself as he fell with relief against the friar's door.

Juliet was here to find a way out of her marriage to Paris. He was grateful Romeo had left before he had a chance to tell him that Juliet was going to marry Paris. With Romeo safe in Mantua, Benvolio had to help Juliet find a way to keep her marriage to Romeo. Then, once they had succeeded, he would be able to go to Mantua and tell Romeo the beautiful truth about everything. He stood and brushed his hair with his hands, but it fell back into his eyes. He knocked on the friar's door to offer his help, but Juliet's scream silenced his knock.

"This shall slay them both," she yelled, her voice cracking with tears.

Benvolio stepped back and looked around to see if anyone was watching him. He knocked again, and again Juliet screamed.

"I long to die."

Her words sent shivers through Benvolio. Her pain was desperate. He wanted in. He opened the door quietly as their voices softened. The friar had calmed her, and he was bringing her to her feet.

Benvolio saw her face. She had stopped crying and was full of hope. They must have found a way to fix it all. He stepped out of the doorway and let them pass. He decided he would tell the friar that he wanted to help with their plan after Juliet left.

"All right then," the friar said to Juliet. "Go home and be happy with your choice here today. Tell your father that you give your consent to marry Paris."

Juliet's face was still full of light and joy. Benvolio didn't understand. He backed up around the corner.

"Benvolio?" Rosaline's sweet voice called to him.

He turned to her.

"What is it, Ben?" she asked. "Has something else happened?"

"I thought Juliet had found a way to remain as Romeo's wife," he said. "I thought they were fixing it."

"Benvolio, what are you talking about? You are white as a ghost."

"Paris."

"The prince's kin?"

"Yes, he is going to marry Juliet this Thursday."

"The friar won't agree to this."

"That's what I thought too."

"What did the friar tell you? He can't marry them, Benvolio, not in the eyes of God."

"It isn't what he told me. It's what he told Juliet."

Rosaline started toward the friar's door. "He can't allow Juliet to be damned by a second marriage while her first husband is still alive," she said.

The friar was walking Juliet out of the church. "Now go home, Juliet," he said. "Be strong and believe in your choice here today. I'll send a friar to Mantua to tell Romeo of your choice."

"Love, give me strength; and strength, give me help. Farewell, dear friar," Juliet said as she left with a smile.

"I don't understand," Rosaline said. "The friar is going to send Romeo a letter to tell him his wife is marrying another man? After he stood in his own church and married her to Romeo? This isn't really happening."

"I went into the friar's chambers, and I heard him tell Juliet to go home and tell her father that she will be happy to marry Paris. And she was happy, Rose. She had stopped crying and was filled with joy."

"This can't be. She could not bury her love for her husband and marry another man so soon."

The friar's voice boomed in the main hall. "We must prepare for a wedding this coming Thursday for the young Lady Juliet to Paris."

"Benvolio, what do we do? This ruins everything. Oh, how can I only think of myself at a time like this? This will kill Romeo and damn my cousin's soul."

"We need to stop the letter from getting to Romeo," he said.

"I can do that. I'll stop the letter from getting to Romeo. I'll replace it with nice news of the streets. He will probably send Friar John. I will remind him of a family that is very dear to him, who has not shown up to service in a while. They are on the way out of town toward Mantua. Perhaps he could stop there, and that will keep him busy."

"What would that do?"

"Keep Friar John away from Romeo as long as we can, in case he speaks to Romeo and lets it slip that the Capulets are planning a wedding for their young Juliet. Benvolio, do you know where you need to be now?"

He looked at her.

"You need to go to Mercutio's funeral. Balthazar is waiting for you outside. I saw him follow you here. He will wait for you as long as you need, but you have to go with him to the tomb. And you need to be there for Mercutio. I know what the pain of losing him is causing you. I love you, Benvolio. Go to his funeral, mourn your dear friend, and find strength in the life he led."

Rosaline squeezed his hand and stole a kiss. He wanted her warm lips to never move from his, but they did. She pushed him toward the entrance doors. He walked outside and cringed at the blinding sun. Balthazar put his hand on his shoulder and guided him to the west end of the church toward the hill, where Mercutio was about to be laid to rest.

14

Verona's graveyard stretched wide with green rolling hills and scattered headstones. Under the hills were the tombs designated for families of noble blood. When a member of the prince's family passed away, the town would gather as the body was carried into the royal tomb at the head of the graveyard. The ceremony would take place deep inside the tomb, and only the family of the prince could attend, leaving the townspeople to quietly mourn outside. The body would be left to gracefully decay on top of a stone bed deep within the tomb, and the family who died before them would guide their spirit to heaven.

When Benvolio and Balthazar turned the corner from the church to the graveyard, they saw that the townspeople had gathered at the graveyard gates. The prince was addressing them all.

"Today we bury our kin. Today the Capulets bury theirs. Today the son of Montague is banished. Today the fighting ends. We warned the people of Verona that death was the answer to any who fought in our streets. You answered us with blood. We will answer back. Mercutio will not begin his eternal life within our family's tomb. He will be buried in a common grave at the top of this hill. Lord Capulet, we hope you do the same with the body of young Tybalt."

In front of the crowd, Lord Capulet stood beside Lady Capulet, who was still crying desperately for the loss of Tybalt. Lord Capulet's head fell in obedience, but Lady Capulet's did not.

The people of Verona began their hike to the top of the hill in the graveyard. Benvolio didn't move. His only comfort in losing Mercutio was knowing that his eternal soul would be guided to heaven by his family members who had died before him.

"Come on, Benvolio," Balthazar said, softly leading him to the path. "I know what you're afraid of, and you don't need to be. Mercutio will find his way to heaven. My father is buried at the top of this hill, and I know he found his way to heaven. He will help Mercutio find his way there as well."

Balthazar's beliefs calmed Benvolio. He began to ascend the steep hill to the grave site. As they got closer to the grave, he could hear the weeping. He could feel the sorrow and the pain inside him grow. He could feel Mercutio's soul leaving his body again. He could see his chest sink and the bottle of brandy fall to the ground. Benvolio grabbed the closest tree and held himself up with its twisted branches. He didn't want to get any closer to the grave. Balthazar stood beside him, and quietly they listened to the funeral.

The ceremony ended, and all the people hiked back down the hill, passing them without a word or a look. The sun was bending down and shining through the trees. Benvolio stood, as did Balthazar, staring up at the site of Mercutio's grave. Balthazar was the first to move. He hiked to the top of the hill and looked at the deep grave. He picked up a handful of dirt and gently tossed it in. He said a quiet prayer and came back down the hill to Benvolio.

"I'll leave you to make your peace with him, Benvolio, but I won't go far," Balthazar said.

Balthazar's footsteps were loud in the gravel until only quiet was left behind. The silence frustrated Benvolio. It was too quiet; he could hear his heart pounding. He moved from the tree and shuffled his feet on the path so the gravel would make noise. He hiked up the steep hillside, taking each step slowly, deciding where to put his foot, what tree to hold for support, blinking as the last bit of sun flickered in his eye through the leaves. He noticed the change in ground as he got closer to the grave.

There was a mound of wet dug-up dirt, wider and taller than his friend was. He lifted his foot and pushed against the mound, leaving a footprint. He stood there and stared at the mound until it became too dark to see the print. Then he got closer, falling to his knees. He could feel the moisture soak through his pants. His body fell to the side, and he turned his back on the grave, leaning against the mound of dirt. His hand sunk into it as he grasped the dirt tight in his fist. His breathing stopped, and he tried to focus on the treetops swaying in the summer breeze. His eyes became blurry with tears. He tightened his grip on the dirt, but it fell through his fingers. The sound of his laughter hit the air and made him jump.

"There has never been silence with you, Mercutio."

Benvolio felt his chest lighten, and he started to breathe again. He lay beside the grave and looked at the yellowing sky.

"I chose not to tell you about Romeo and Juliet because I knew you would be a dankish, hasty-witted coxcomb, and I was right to think that. You would have tormented Romeo like you did me with Rosaline. I actually believed that Romeo's blind love for our enemy's daughter could be strong enough to end this fight. I didn't want you to mess with him."

Benvolio turned and looked at the grave for the first time. It was a dark hole. The little bit of dirt thrown in was not enough to cover the wooden box that held his friend. He tried not to think about the dead body inside the box. He looked down at his hands. They were filthy. He wrung them together, feeling the scratch of the dirt against his dry skin.

Benvolio

"Romeo will die now too, you realize. Juliet was a traitor. She was tested, and she failed. She gave up so easily, and now she will do as her father tells her. Here I am, worried about your eternal soul while she will be married to two men come Thursday. I'll drink to her damned soul rotting in hell."

He went to raise his glass, but the sight of his dirty empty hand brought him back. His hand fell, and he looked back at the grave.

"I asked you not to fight with Tybalt. I might not have given you the truth or all the information, but I asked you not to fight him. But you wanted to fight him, didn't you? You got excited talking about it. You wanted to fight in our fight. You knew Tybalt well enough to know that he was out for blood. You were always sick that way, open to sudden death. I should have seen that the pain inside you was strong enough to make you want to fight him."

Benvolio stood up and stepped away from the grave. "Oh, Mercutio, were you actually in that much pain? Or were you just that big a fool to think angering Tybalt would end well for you?"

Benvolio stopped. He could hear music rise from the bottom of the hill. He walked to the edge of the grave site and looked down at the entrance of the graveyard. The Capulets were burying Tybalt in their family tomb, defying the humble request of the prince and giving Tybalt a proper burial.

"Typical Capulets, might as well bury him with honor because he didn't live with any," he said.

He turned back to Mercutio's grave and took his seat against the mound of dirt. The music became louder as the Capulets made their way toward their tomb. He could hear weeping and softly spoken prayers. The music took on an eerie twang as it entered the deep halls of the tomb and faded, along with the cries and prayers of the family.

Benvolio sat still and silent for a very long time until his eyes drifted to the sky. He focused eventually on the moon. He knew what time it was. This was always the time to sneak out of the house and into the woods to meet Rosaline.

"I never really told you about those nights, Mercutio," Benvolio said. His voice broke the silence again, but it comforted him to talk. "The day I chased her into the woods, Rosaline asked me to meet her back there every night. Did I ever tell you how I met her? No, because this is the first time you let me get a word in, isn't it?"

Benvolio put his hands behind his head, and a smile came across his face. "This is nice. Maybe if you'd shut up every once in a while…well, you can't punch me with the butt of your sword now, can you? You gave me my first black eye, remember that? Romeo and I had just turned ten, I think, and my uncle was going to throw a huge party. When everyone arrived, Romeo and I went looking for you. We had just received our wooden swords. We had no idea what to do with them yet, but we wanted to show them off to you so badly. When we found you, you already had a real sword. You told us to draw and fight, so we did. That fight was epic. We chased each other through the crowds and angered my aunt and uncle. I called you a fawning, dog-hearted harpy. I should have always left the insults up to you. Anyway, you punched me with the butt of your sword right in the eye. Then, as if it were no big deal, you and Romeo continued fighting, but damn, it hurt."

Benvolio closed his eyes. In silence, he sat by his friend, listening to the birds sing and dance in the trees. The night was very old when he heard footsteps approaching him. He opened his eyes and saw a gaggle of nuns hiking up the hill. He was ending this day as he had ended the last: lying next to death as the nuns came to clean away the sight of it all.

"I thought you might still be here," Rosaline said.

The nuns began to work around the grave, picking up after the weeping patrons who had left behind their tear-filled rags and trash. Rosaline hitched up her black robe and sat beside him. Benvolio looked to the nuns for approval, but none would look his way.

"Have you eaten?" Rosaline asked.

"I—Rose, I miss him, and I miss Romeo. I miss you," Benvolio said. He could not look at her, so he kept his eyes on his hands.

"I'm right here beside you, Ben."

"In the cemetery."

"I was able to stop the letter the friar sent to Romeo." She handed him the original letter. "I replaced it, and Friar John will be stopping at the home of the family that has not come to service for a while. I told him I would let Friar Lawrence know he was making an extrastop so he wouldn't tell him. I hope it will also keep him from returning before the wedding to report that Romeo was not offended by the letter and make Friar Lawrence question anything."

Benvolio took the original letter and put it in his pocket. He reached for her hand and held it tight, feeling her soft skin. "Thank you, Rose."

"I never got the chance to thank you for the flowers," she said with a smile.

He looked down.

"Benvolio," she continued, pulling his head to her. "You need to go home. I want you to eat and sleep and know that you are not alone today. Today your aunt and uncle have lost their son to Mantua. Your place is with them now, not here at this dark grave alone."

"My aunt and uncle had the chance to end this fight, you know. They could have never told us about it. They could have punished us and their servants every time we fought in the streets. Now it's too late. We all have to live with their choice to continue fighting."

Rosaline took her hand from his and got to her knees.

"Aren't you a man, Benvolio?" she asked. "Don't you choose your own moves and make your own mistakes?

You are angry with your aunt and uncle. I understand that, but don't put all the blame on them. You drew your sword against Tybalt as well."

Benvolio's head fell into his hands. "I've destroyed everything."

"You've worked very hard to destroy everything, but you haven't succeeded. As long as you are breathing, I will always love you."

"Am I breathing now?"

"I'll send Balthazar to you with some bread and wine. You need to eat, but I understand you won't leave this place right now. You have lost a lot in one day, but, Benvolio, you haven't lost me."

As she kissed his cheek, Benvolio closed his eyes. His heart fluttered, and the night's cold air soothed him. His mind and body were tired. He heard Rosaline rise beside him. He looked up at her as Sister Mary Margaret took her by the arm and led her away from the grave site and back down the hillside. He listened to their footsteps in the gravel, but the awful silence filled the air once again. It buzzed in his ears until he let his head fall back onto the cool mound of dirt.

15

He woke up to the sound of the lark singing peacefully above him. The sun was well into the sky, and a loaf of bread was on his lap. He tore at it with his dirty hands and shoved a large piece into his dry mouth. He looked around. Beside him was a bottle of wine standing on the dirt. He pulled the cork out with his teeth, spit it into the woods, and took a long swig. He moved and stretched and remembered where he was. He stood up and threw a chunk of bread into Mercutio's grave, followed by a healthy stream of wine.

"Farewell, my good friend. You will be in my heart every day as you were by my side throughout my life," he said, taking a drink to honor his friend.

Music was making its way up the hill. Benvolio's light heart sank once more. He couldn't imagine who had died now. He stumbled to the edge of the grave. It was the Capulets again. They had gathered and were walking toward their tomb. Benvolio ran to the path and descended partway down the hill to see who the Capulets were burying. The Capulet colors were flooding the graveyard, coupled with sheets, shields, and silks of black.

"Please, God, don't let it be Rosaline," he whispered.

Leading the procession was Lord Capulet, Rosaline's uncle. Benvolio took a deep breath. It wasn't Rosaline. He saw Lady Capulet, Juliet's mother, weeping a little less desperately than when she buried Tybalt. She was surrounded by many people, including Paris, who was weeping as well. A branch broke behind Benvolio, making him jump.

"Balthazar, you scared me. Who is it? Which Capulet is dead?" Benvolio asked.

"It is Juliet Capulet," Balthazar said. "Their only daughter. The Capulets are finally getting what they deserve."

"What happened? Did one of us kill her?"

"No, Benvolio, she died of a broken heart."

"She what? What are you saying?"

"The loss of Tybalt was too much for her to bear."

"Tybalt? Right."

Benvolio dropped his bread and ran down the hill.

"Benvolio, where are you going?"

Without answering, Benvolio got as close to the procession as he could. He saw the weeping eyes of Rosaline and her family. On the cold slab, draped in black silk, was the young and beautiful Juliet. Her dark hair lay over her shoulders. Her white face was lifeless, as Mercutio's was, as Tybalt's was. Their souls were gone forever.

Benvolio fell to his knees. Romeo would not be able to survive this news alone in Mantua. Standing at the opening of the tomb, the friar was looking directly at Benvolio with terrifying concern.

"You're right to be afraid of me, old man," Benvolio said quietly. "Balthazar," he yelled up the hill.

"I'm right here," Balthazar said behind him.

"Oh, right. Listen to me. I need you to do something very important for me, and I can't tell you why."

"Why are you so upset about Juliet Capulet's death?"

"Listen to me. I need you to go to Mantua and bring back Romeo. Bring him straight to me at Mercutio's grave. Don't let him go home. Don't let him go anywhere or talk to anyone or be seen. Do you understand me?"

"I do."

"Go now, please. Be fast."

"Come with me, Benvolio. You need to get away from this place."

"I can't. There's a chance Romeo will get here before you get to him. I need to be here if he comes."

"Fine, I'll go now and bring Romeo to you."

Balthazar ran out of the graveyard, and Benvolio looked back for the friar. He and the Capulet family had disappeared into their tomb. Benvolio realized he was a fool for doubting Juliet's love for Romeo. She died of a broken heart, but no one else knew it was for her banished husband. That look of resolve on her face when the friar told her to marry Paris was because she had decided to die.

16

Benvolio hiked back up the hill to Mercutio's grave. From there, he could see the entrance to the Capulet tomb, as well as the entrance to the graveyard. He would make sure he was the first person to see Romeo when he came back.

The graveyard was almost peaceful with the Capulets deep in their tomb. The birds sang in the trees above him, and they sounded cheerful. It was confusing to Benvolio. He took a seat and rested his head on the tree beside him, keeping his eyes open for Romeo. He thought about Rosaline. She had come to comfort him in his loss, and he would make sure to do the same tonight after Romeo was safe at home. Quietly the Capulet family began to come out of the tomb. The friar stepped into the sun and took a look around. Benvolio knew he was looking for him.

"You won't stop me from making this right, old man," Benvolio whispered.

Benvolio

The friar walked out of the cemetery. The Capulets were holding tightly to one another and softly weeping. Their silence broke when Lady Capulet exited the tomb. Her desperate screams rang through the trees. Rosaline's parents came out together. Her mother wept as if it were her own daughter they had buried. For some reason, Benvolio thought she would have embraced Rosaline in this moment, but they were not together.

The Capulet family was large, and it took time for all of them to clear the tomb. Eventually the family left, and silence came back. But Rosaline had not come out yet. Benvolio's heart began to pound. He could picture her in the tomb alone, in great sorrow over her loss. He understood her pain. He felt himself inching down the hill toward the tomb, knowing he should not go in. But before he could take a proper step, Rosaline came out of the tomb with her fellow nuns. Their heads were down as they marched out of the cemetery.

"I'll come and comfort you tonight, my Rose. You're not alone either."

Moments passed before the sound of the birds hit his ears again. He turned to Mercutio's grave and stared at it. The lack of sleep and not much food was messing with his mind. The day had gone by quickly, and eventually the sun began to set. His nerves started to take over. What was he going to do once Romeo arrived? He needed a plan. He could sneak Romeo into the Capulet tomb to say good-bye to Juliet. He would stand guard as Romeo wept and prayed. Then he would bring him home without being seen by the prince or his men. He could take him out of the cemetery through the woods and walk him around the outskirts of Verona until they hit their land. It would be safe.

And once Romeo's mother and father saw him, they would help console him. They would take care of him and hear of his love for Juliet. All this pain and loss would begin to make sense to them as they witness the love in their son's heart. The understanding Romeo's parents would have could spread through the town, to the prince, to the Capulets. And perhaps peace would eventually exist in Verona once more. Perhaps he would be free to dream of a life with Rosaline. Benvolio's heart sank at the thought. Could he still have hope while Romeo's love was lying dead in a tomb? Could he really be that selfish on the day of Juliet's death?

Benvolio paced around Mercutio's grave, forming a sunken path around it. The sun left the sky, and the dark made it difficult for Benvolio to stay strong. The nightingale began to sing. It had taken over the silence in his mind and calmed him. He went to the edge of the hill to see if Romeo and Balthazar had returned. At the entrance to the Capulet tomb, he saw a freshly lit torch. Fear filled him, and his heart began to race. He took off down the hill to the tomb. He made it halfway down when he could see clearly through the trees. One of the figures was very small and could not be Balthazar, and the other was definitely not Romeo. Benvolio moved silently toward the tomb through the trees, staying hidden. As he got closer, the small man had brought his torch down to the ground to put out its light. Benvolio could plainly see the other man's face. It was Paris.

If Paris were secretly visiting Juliet, Benvolio would have to be very careful with Romeo. This would change his plan drastically. He needed to get back to Mercutio's grave to make sure he didn't miss Romeo when he arrived. He got back to his post and continued to search for the light of another torch. Balthazar would have one to make it to Mercutio's grave. And Paris's page would light his again to find their way out.

"Paris, you poor fool," Benvolio said to himself.

After a while, he heard a voice threaten a man not to follow him back into the tomb. Benvolio sighed.

"Say your good-byes and leave, Paris. You never had her heart, and you have no right to be by her side tonight."

Paris's page relit his torch. Their voices grew, and with their volume, Benvolio heard the clanking of swords.

He ran down the hill through the trees to stay hidden. The flame of the torch was lighting up two fighting figures. As he got closer, he saw that the torch was being held by a third man. He ran faster through the trees. As Benvolio got closer to them, the small man holding the torch started to run out of the graveyard, leaving the fighters in pitch-black.

"Oh, Lord, they're fighting. I'll go call for help," the man yelled.

Benvolio ran closer to the clanging of the swords, blind to every root and branch in his way, until his feet failed him. With a terrible fall, his head bounced off a rock, and his breath was pushed out of his chest. The trees above him danced in the wind. The stars sparkled a little brighter, and the cold earth soothed him as it always had. He smiled and decided to stay where he had fallen. It was so pretty there. His eyes felt heavy, so he let them close.

"Benvolio?" Balthazar yelled, shaking him awake.

"Balthazar, what is it?" Benvolio said, coughing.

"I've been looking for you in the dark. Why are you sleeping in the trees?"

"In the what?"

"I've brought Romeo home, like you asked."

Benvolio sat up and rubbed his head. He felt the earth below him and heard the birds around him and remembered how he ended up sleeping in the trees. "There was a fight," Benvolio said.

He jumped to his feet and looked around. They were standing at the edge of the woods on the main path to the Capulet tomb. There were no more fighting men, only him and Balthazar.

"You brought Romeo home?" Benvolio asked. "Where is he?"

"I was trying to bring him to you at Mercutio's grave, but the moment we arrived, he went straight into the Capulet tomb. I told him Mercutio was buried on the top of the hill, but I think he was confused. He's been acting strangely ever since I told him Juliet Capulet died."

"He is in the Capulet tomb now?"

"Yes."

"Balthazar, why didn't you—come on, we have to go."

"Benvolio, wait. You're covered in dirt. You fell down the hill, didn't you? Did you hit your head? Look at me. Let me see your eyes."

"They're brown like a cow's," Benvolio said.

"You're acting strangely."

"I can't bury Romeo. Come on."

"Benvolio, wait, no. Why would we go into the Capulet tomb? Why the hell would we bury Romeo? Please tell me what's going on."

"I have to go in there now and—"

"Benvolio, I just spoke to the friar. Please calm down and listen to me. Romeo will soon realize that Mercutio isn't in there. He will come back out, and we will be able to take him up the hill to Mercutio's grave and explain everything to him. But you can't go in there after him."

"I'm going."

"Stop."

"I can't, Balthazar."

"Ben, stop, please. Romeo is acting strangely. When we got to the graveyard gates, he threatened to punish me if I let anyone follow him into that tomb."

"That was Romeo?"

"Yes, he closed the gates on me and locked them from inside. I tried to tell him where Mercutio was, that you were waiting for him. He told me to wait at the gate. I watched him head for the Capulet tombs. I wasn't able to get to you, so I went to get the friar. He unlocked the gates, and I sent him after Romeo, and I came to find you. Look, Romeo's not himself. It will be fine if we just wait for him here."

"The friar is in the tomb with him now?"

"Yes."

"The friar isn't the man you think he is. He doesn't care about Romeo. Give me your torch."

"Yes, sir," Balthazar said angrily as he handed over the torch. "What is with you and Romeo, Ben?"

"Wait here for us, please. We will need to get Romeo home before anyone else sees him back in Verona."

"I'll be here."

Benvolio ran into the dark halls of the Capulet tomb. The fire of his torch flickered against a wet pool of blood. He knew it was from the fight he'd heard. He made his way toward the heart of the tomb, and as the light filled the hallway, he saw the friar running toward him.

"Benvolio?"

"Friar, did you find Romeo?"

"Benvolio, why did you bring him back here? Oh God, I'm so very sorry for my part in this."

The friar pushed Benvolio away and ran out of the tomb. Benvolio was scared, but he moved forward. The funeral candles were still lit in the large room at the end of the hall. He looked in and saw they were all placed around Juliet. She looked like a peaceful angel. The flickering light of the candles gave movement to her lifeless body. He heard a voice sing through the tunnel. He stopped. The voice was coming from Juliet's direction. It was soft, sweet, and sad.

"Your lips are warm," it said.

"Juliet?" Benvolio said breathlessly.

Juliet's body sat straight up. She was alive. He ran to her. The closer he got, he could see her looking down at someone. Romeo? Of course, she was looking at Romeo, who lay in her arms. She was kissing him. Could he truly be seeing his cousin in the arms of his living love? He turned to leave when his light hit the dead body of Paris, who was propped up against the cold stone wall.

"Oh no," Benvolio whispered.

"Which way?" a loud voice called from the entrance of the tomb.

"Romeo," Benvolio whispered. "Romeo, I'm sorry, but we have to get out of here."

He turned back, and his light flickered off a silver dagger. Juliet was holding it above her with both hands. Tears dropped from her cheeks. Her breast rose with breath, and she quickly pushed the dagger into her chest.

"Juliet!" Benvolio screamed, running to her.

But her last gaze was for Romeo. She fell onto him. He was not moving.

"Romeo?" Benvolio called out. He ran to them. He could hear the men behind him approaching fast, but he didn't care. "Romeo?" he yelled. He grabbed his cousin's body and shook it. "Romeo!" he screamed.

Juliet's dead body was intertwined with Romeo's. The noises from the hallway were becoming louder and jumbled. The light dimmed, and his legs gave way. His eyes could make nothing out except two hands held together, falling from the slab above him. He allowed his eyes to close. It brought him peace, until the light pried his eyes open, and loud voices filled the stone room. He blinked, trying to understand where he was, what was going on around him. He saw Balthazar being pushed into the bright room. He could tell that two of the prince's watchmen were pushing him. Benvolio could hear them accusing Balthazar, questioning him about the deaths. Benvolio couldn't let Balthazar be punished for what happened.

He willed himself to stand and go speak for him, but his legs wouldn't move. His arms wouldn't move. His head began to spin, and again, all he could feel was the hard floor beneath him. He tried to take a deep breath. So much had been lost, and he knew he was not the only one who felt this way. He had to find the strength to fight for what he still had. The air became dusty, and Benvolio realized he had been joined by many people inside the tomb. He could see the friar standing scared in the corner. Benvolio got to his knees and made his way out from under the slab that held his cousin's body. He went to the wall and used it to help him stay standing. He started to walk toward Balthazar, but he saw the Capulets come rushing in. There was confusion on their faces as they saw their daughter, newly bleeding, with Romeo in her arms.

Benvolio stepped forward to speak, but he was stopped by a warm, familiar voice. His uncle had arrived. Benvolio moved along the wall. He knew the pain of losing a son to death would break a man, even one as strong as his uncle. He needed to stand with him.

The prince asked Lord Montague to come closer to the deathbed. His uncle began to speak as he approached Romeo's and Juliet's bodies. "My prince, my wife is dead tonight," Lord Montague said.

Benvolio fell back onto the wall. His aunt was dead, gone in her grief. She had passed away in her mourning for her banished son as Benvolio sat at Mercutio's grave, not willing to go home to comfort her. He could have explained it all to her, let her know why her son was banished, why he would kill a man like Tybalt. But he hadn't gone home, and now she too was dead. Benvolio looked up to see the strong figure of his uncle collapse before Romeo's body.

The prince yelled out a demand to know what had happened. Benvolio opened his mouth to tell everything he knew, but the friar stepped forward and spoke first. Benvolio had to make it to his uncle. He knew Balthazar would be cleared by the friar's story, and all would know whose fault this truly was. And he knew his uncle needed him most of all. He silently made his way through the crowd. He helped his uncle to his feet, and with his shoulders, he kept him standing. As the friar spoke of Romeo and Juliet's love for each other, his uncle looked at him in disbelief.

"I assure you, Uncle, their love was true," Benvolio said.

"Juliet came to my cell," the friar said. "She was crying about her arranged marriage to Paris. She told me with wild eyes that if she were to lose her soul and her marriage to her love, she would kill herself in my cell at that moment. So I gave her a sleeping potion that would give the illusion of death."

Benvolio turned to the friar. "A sleeping potion?"

The friar continued, "She took it last night. You found her this morning, thinking she was dead, and you placed her here. Meanwhile, I had written a letter to Romeo. It told him of our plan, and he was to come home at the moment she woke to take her from this place. They were going to leave together and live and love forever in Mantua, but Romeo never received the letter."

"The letter?" Benvolio said.

Benvolio

He held on to his uncle with one hand and reached into his pocket with the other. As all ears were on the friar, Benvolio opened the letter and read it. It didn't tell Romeo about Juliet's wedding to Paris—it was all about the friar's plan. Benvolio realized his interference had ruined everything. He had killed Romeo, Juliet, Paris, and his aunt.

The friar continued to speak, and once he was finished, Balthazar began to explain his part in the tragedy. Benvolio wanted to speak. He tried, but nothing came out. What was he going to say? That he had drawn his sword against Tybalt in peace? He had let Mercutio fight Tybalt to save Romeo? He had let Romeo fight Tybalt out of pure rage then abandoned his aunt and uncle in their time of grief? He had taken the letter that could have saved his cousin. He had fallen asleep beneath a tree in the dark woods of the graveyard as Romeo killed Paris in the tomb and then killed himself. And he had stood there and watched as Juliet took her own life.

Benvolio knew he had to step forward and say it all, but before him, he saw the hand of his uncle firmly shake the hand of Lord Capulet. He didn't know what just happened. His uncle was walking out of the tomb with Lord Capulet arm in arm, and eventually everyone was gone.

The candles were the only light. He stood there alone, staring at the bodies of Romeo and Juliet. The light flickered, causing the shadows on the deathbeds to dance around.

Emily Whitaker

Voices started to come again from the hall. He turned and saw the nuns coming in with their heads down.

Benvolio looked at each of them. None of them were Rosaline. He hoped they would ignore him as they had done before. They prayed as they arranged Romeo's and Juliet's bodies. They placed them peacefully together on the stone slab. The nuns moved about the tomb, relighting candles that had burnt out. Each nun silently took her leave from the tomb but one, Sister Mary Margaret. She took her place beside Benvolio. She gently grabbed his hand and whispered one last prayer. She let the silence fill the air and turned to Benvolio.

"I knew when I took Rosaline in that her heart belonged to you, Benvolio," she said. "She has never been on the path to join our sisterhood. I knew that, and still I took her in with open, loving arms. I did this because I believe in the love she has for you. I truly believe it is strong enough to warm her mother's heart and help her see the joy love can bring instead of hate. But this love between you needed time. It was my hope to give that to you by bringing her into the church, by keeping her from her mother's influence and allowing the love between you both to flourish. I just saw your uncle leave this tomb holding the hand of her uncle. My dear child, I know you are filled with pain at this moment, but you must see the light your love for her can bring. Find your strength and go to her. It is time.

She is waiting for you to shake her father's hand at the Capulet villa."

Sister Mary Margaret let go of Benvolio's hand and left peacefully. He was frozen by her words. He needed to find the strength that had filled him only days ago to shake the hand of Rosaline's father. He needed to go to her, but he couldn't make his feet walk away from Romeo. He could see his own chest rising with his breath. He pushed to keep it moving, sucking all the air he could into his lungs. And with the air, the darkness began to fade.

"Where is he?" a voice screeched down the hall of the tomb.

Benvolio's head twisted to the entrance.

Rosaline's mother came screaming into the room. Her dress was sparkling gracefully against the candlelight. Her voice hit Benvolio like a slap on the face.

"You coward, you will never marry my daughter," she cried as she came at him with her trusty dagger in hand.

Benvolio stepped toward her, grabbed her wrist, and twisted the dagger to her side.

"Excuse me, madam," he said. "You know about my love for your daughter?"

"Yes, she told me, and it sickens me."

"Then you cannot stop me now. You will not come at me with a dagger as I stand at the feet of our dead family lying together for eternity. You will not spill any more blood in the name of this fight because it is over now."

Benvolio stepped forward, pushing her back, keeping the dagger pointed away from him at her side. "I have done many things to be undeserving of your daughter, but being a Montague is not one of them. In my desire to stop this fight, I have killed many, and so have you. You are no better than I am, and you are no worse. So I suggest you drop this dagger and take my hand. Walk with me out of this tomb and into the cemetery yards, where my uncle stands hand in hand with your brother. I suggest that you announce your desire to have your daughter marry me because you have learned of our love and accept it. Drop the dagger, madam. Drop it for your daughter, or if you will not, then drop it for your brother, who will have your head if you go against his word."

Lady Capulet dropped the dagger. Benvolio took her hand. It felt dry and crusty. He pushed her away to get a better look at her. It was not her dress that sparkled in the candlelight; it was blood. She was soaked in it.

"I could not have her marrying a Montague," she said.

"Rosaline?" Benvolio said. "What did you do to her?" He pushed Lady Capulet to the ground.

He ran into the dark hall, but he was stopped immediately. His legs wouldn't move, and the ground was slowly getting closer. He looked down at the silver blade that was slicing through his shirt. It was covered in blood, his blood. His breathing stopped to let out a cough that sprayed a red cloud in front of him. Lady Capulet came and stood over him.

"Well done, Gregory," she said.

Gregory came from behind Benvolio and took Lady Capulet's arm.

"Now," she continued. "Escort me out of this dreadful place so I may stand next to my brother in peace."

They turned and walked away.

"Rosaline," Benvolio said, coughing.

"Yes, you can have her now," Lady Capulet said as she left him to die alone in the dark halls of the Capulet family tombs.